Peace in the Midst

Unexpected Gifts Series
Book 1

by
T.W.Allgaier

Peace in the Midst, **a novel from the** *Unexpected Gift* **Series**, is entirely a work of fiction and of this author's imagination. Where real people, dead or alive, or specific events, businesses, organizations or locations appear, they are intended only to give the fiction a sense of reality and authenticity.

Copyright © 2018 T.W.Allgaier
ISBN: 9781730889301

~TO~

My husband, Alphonse, the love of my life. Thank you for listening to me talk about my dreams for almost 43 years.

You have a servant's heart and I love you with all of mine. Sometimes the circumstances in our lives have been difficult, but without you and Jesus by my side, I would not have made it through any of them. I would not want to do life with anyone else.

My sons and daughters-in-law, whose lives reflect true love in every aspect of the word. Watching you all become wonderful adults has been a joy.

And watching two of you parent your daughter is nothing less than beautiful.

My Mom, who rose to each challenge in her life with love and grace and continues to do so. Thank you for being you. Love you.

My maternal grandmother, whose zeal and tenacity for life carried her through many things. Her love for her Lord was an example to me as I grew up.

She let me paint her nails, read her *Reader's Digest* and watch *Lawerence Welk.* We stayed up late to eat popcorn and drink 7-Up ice cream sodas too many nights to count.

My paternal grandmother, whose strength I admired. Her love for me as I became an adult helped me to believe that I could do what I was called to do and that nothing could stop me.

My sweet friends and family who have encouraged me along the way. Some have read the book in its infancy, others helped edit and others were there to push me along. You know who you are and you are all treasures to me!

My precious grandchild.....Sweet little girl, you are our first grandchild. I love you with all my heart, and look forward to watching you become the person God designed you to be.

And thank you to my loving Lord and Savior, Jesus Christ. You gave me the desire to encourage others. There are so many difficult situations in life, and encouragement is desperately needed.

The circumstances have often swirled in my own life....but you, my Lord, have never left me, and I know you never will.

"I have told you these things, so that in Me you may have [perfect] peace. In the world you will have tribulation and distress and suffering, but be courageous [be confident, be undaunted, be filled with joy]; I have overcome the world." [My conquest is accomplished, My victory abiding.] John 16:33 (AMP)

CHAPTER 1
1981

We started having issues in our marriage several years ago. And yes, I will admit it does take two and there are always "two sides to every story," but when I found out that Mark was having an affair…well, let's just say that it would take more than a couple of counseling sessions to fix that.

I was hurt, and it wasn't just my husband that betrayed me. My friends knew as well! How could that have happened? How do you ever get over that?

I confided in my friends about Mark almost every time we talked. This was my mistake. They knew about the affair and never bothered to mention it.

He doesn't pay any attention to me," I said time and time again. "He just doesn't care about my feelings," I told the two of them. "The romance is gone and I don't know what to do anymore". How many times at coffee did I "spill" the beans? Sorry for the pun.

And there you have it. Both Mark and the other woman were unhappy and supposedly it "just happened" and was a horrible mistake. I'd say.

I am sure she knew how to get him to pay attention, how to get him to care about her feelings…and I am sure she worked the romance in somehow.

I know he was not simply seduced by her. He was taking part in it as well. My blood boils just thinking about it. And after I got over the anger, I replaced it with sheer pain. I became simply numb from it all….and I still was.

Mark had wanted to stay and work it out. He asked for forgiveness. "I'll work on that," I told him before I said I had already seen a lawyer. Mark had given me a Biblical reason for divorce, and I was taking it.

My heart was broken in several pieces. I was not happy. Oh, I know that they always say the "grass is not always greener," but I figured if it were even brown and dormant it was alive. It was worth trying.

The counselor had earned her fee. She tried to show us how we needed to appreciate each other, focus on forgiveness and she said all those other things counselors say. I listened. Mark was remorseful.

"No excuse" was my standard reply. And truthfully, Biblically...there was not. I knew it, he knew it and the counselor knew it. I had an excuse to get out of the marriage.

Mark had no fight left in him and was so full of guilt that there was no contest for the divorce. Another few weeks, and our 22 plus year marriage was over.

The kids were devastated, but I knew they would be okay. They begged us to stay together and then they begged us to get back together.

"Kids, you just don't understand" I always replied. I could not tell them what happened and demean their father. I would not disrupt that relationship. Mark was an incredible father and that was worth saving for our kids.

The "other woman" also asked for forgiveness. No counselor needed for that one. "You were someone I saw every day when I dropped the kids off for school, not to mention that we were homeroom mothers together for years!"

I sobbed as we talked on the front porch one. "How could you?" The "other woman" was miserable.

"It just happened."

Well, I had heard that before. I could not even fathom it "just happening." When it was "happening" were they even thinking of me...the wife, the "homeroom mother?" Guess not. Really? Of course, they were not!

Sin is indeed pleasurable for a moment, and in this case over a year! I could not even let my kids get together with her kids anymore. It was just too hard.

We won't even talk about the so-called "friends" who knew about the affair. I know now that they weren't really my friends. Oh, I know it would be hard to tell me the news that would potentially destroy me and my marriage, but wasn't there something to be said about honesty and true friendship?

Who were they really worried about hurting? They had seen them together, knew the truth and never told me. Nothing, not even a hint as to what was going on.

I felt like my heart was surrounded by a circular ten-foot wall. The fact that our marriage was not healthy and the fact that things had happened over several years built that wall brick by brick. Add to the wall the affair and that it had lasted almost a year...let's just say the bricks were mortared in pretty well!

The thought of a relationship of any kind....whether a friend, boyfriend or husband was off the table. Another dog would be the only possibility I would consider, maybe even a cat. That in itself was evidence of my pain. I did not like cats at all.

I was not interested in doing anything but raising my children and running the bakery successfully. The kids did not deserve this type of hurt.

No, I was going to live the remainder of my life being a single mom who happened to be a great baker and busi-nesswoman.

I thought my pies were sweeter than my disposition. But one of my employees disagreed one day.

"Mattie, look…you are a great boss and I love working here. But…."

"But what?" I said as I sprinkled the powdered sugar on the freshly baked cherry pie.

"I know you are hurting, but that bitter stuff you are carrying around inside of you is spilling out on the pie, even that powdered sugar isn't helping," Norah said.

She was right.

CHAPTER 2
1981

I had decided that I needed to take another day off from the bakery. The crew could do without their owner one more day. The slump in the economy had taken its toll on the bakery business, but thankfully I could still call "E.A's Bakery" a success. Local businesses were supported so well in the community.

I had added sugar cookies, brownies, and special order cakes to the menu. Once I added the coffee, donuts, pastries and opened before dawn, it became more of a place for people to come and start their day. It was the added cushion I needed.

My aunt would have been proud. Mother got to see the success before she passed away. Unfortunately, although I tried to keep it from her, she saw the pain of the divorce as well. Some things you just can't hide from your mom….they can almost pull the stuff right out of your mouth, no matter how old you are!

I started the bakery in college with money my aunt had left me, along with a small sum from mother and daddy and an anonymous donor. Although I asked over and over, no one would tell me who this secret person was…just that I was loved, which I already knew.

My aunt had taught me how to make pies. She made the best pies in the area and only shared her recipe with me and my cousins. My cousins had other interests and were a bit older than me, but baking became my love.

She also helped me come up with my own recipes. My sugar cookies did not start out so well, but now people special ordered them.

She taught me how to decorate cakes and use fresh ingredients. She was simply amazing and a wonderful aunt and teacher.

Maybe it was because I did not have any brothers and sisters myself. Maybe it was because it was just me and my mom. My Dad had passed away when I was just a little girl. But whatever the reason, I loved to bake and make people happy with sweet tasting desserts.

I would run to my aunt's kitchen every chance I got. Her kitchen smelled of cherries, apples, and blueberries.

"What are we baking today?" I would shout as I ran in the door. She would already have the pans and bowls on the table, ready for my concoctions.

I learned to listen at her house. She never wrote down her recipes and would remind me that I needed to listen closely so I wouldn't miss anything. That was something that I was not the best at…listening.

"My, my," my precious aunt would say while biting into my latest pie. I waited with anticipation hoping for her approval.

One time I remember being so excited about a new blackberry pie I had made for the first time. I just knew it would be delicious. I took a huge bite.

"Yuck" came out of my mouth almost as quick as the bite. "This is awful!" I uttered as I placed the bite in my napkin.

"Hmmmmm….wondered what part of the recipe you did not hear because of your constant chattering this afternoon?" Well, I learned my lesson.

Mark did not try to get any part of the bakery in the divorce since I started it with that gift from my aunt, my parents, and a "mysterious friend." Somehow I felt I might learn who it was someday, but I was not sure how.

Mark's welding shop was doing well and I did not want any part of it either. Unbelievably, maybe miraculously, it all had worked out. God was still a part of my life after all. He still loved me. Didn't He? *I do love you, Mattie.*

I thought I heard that, but for the first time in a long time, I actually questioned Him. No one else seemed to love me, how could I still be sure that God did? I knew He did not mind questions and was not surprised at all by my doubt.

The three kids were finally at Barlow Youth Camp, and I was hopeful that a "normalcy" of some kind would return to our lives.

"Normal" I uttered under my breath as I set out to conquer the herculean task of going through the mail. That had always been Mark's job. We used to race to the mailbox to see who got to it first, I always loved to tease him. Well, that race would not ever run again. I guess I "won."

Buster, our terrier, sat at my feet, begging for some attention. "Oh boy, this might be a long week," I thought. Buster would be without his playmates and would remind Mattie often.

Skimming through the mail I noticed a large envelope. "That's strange" I muttered to myself, "most of Mother's friends are gone." I noticed that the address was written in a shaky cursive script. For some reason, it felt important.

Little did I know...

CHAPTER 3
1940

The weather matched Esther's mood. High humidity and cold lemonade did not provide the usual cooling effect. She stood from her chair to look out the window and check on the children.

A huge dark cloud was approaching and she knew it was time to call them in. The cloud looked like a wall and like nothing she had ever seen.

The cellar was ready for use, but not the place Esther really wanted to spend the afternoon, she had so much to do. It was stocked with all of her canning supplies and canned goods, so there was not much room for her and the three children.

But the cloud looked fierce and there was no time to waste. The 1940 spring storm season had started off with a bang.

Now that William was gone there was always something to do. The inside work was hard enough to keep up with, but combined with the outside work, Esther did not feel like she got a moment's rest. But what choice did she have?

She was not sure how much longer she could go without help. The neighbors had been so helpful after William's death over a year ago, but they had their own places to tend to and could not go on helping forever.

Farming had been a part of William's life ever since he was a little boy. They rotated their crops, but corn was the cash crop. They also had cows and when the market was good the farm seemed worth it. There were other years when that was hardly the case.

When William's parents passed away, he stayed on to keep the farm going. His two older brothers had headed to discover the "wild west" and had no interest in the farm.

William had first met Esther when she was just in 8th grade. William had quit school before his 9th-grade year when his Pa got sick. He had been working for years now.

He was a few years older than Esther, but it did not seem to bother them. While things were hard enough coming out of the Great Depression, they still courted for five years and fell deeply in love.

Esther was able to graduate from high school and ten days later she married William. That had always been their plan.

"Esther, you will have time for a husband and babies after high school, but I want you to finish." William had always said. She had to agree.

Their marriage was precious and they both worked very hard. Esther taught herself how to make pies and took them to church on Sunday for the dinner on the grounds.

"Esther, this pie is amazing. You must either share the recipe or start selling these tasty things!" said Mrs. Walters one day after church.

The more she heard those kinds of comments, the better the idea sounded. She also knew it would help the family since money was always needed for the farm. She baked for about a year and perfected her pie making ability.

She did get a bit lonely, but that loneliness did not last long. Soon children started coming, the first a bit unexpected.

"William, I think it is time," Esther said one morning as he sat drinking his coffee. He had been up since before sunrise feeding the animals and was just getting ready to go out into the field.

William picked up the telephone. "Myrtle, can you get a hold of Doc Turner? Esther is getting ready to birth this baby!" William knew that Myrtle would spread the news on the telephone party line. "Myrtle, go ahead and ring Anne so she can come and help Esther."

Esther had talked to Anne about being there for the birth. Anne was older than Esther by several years, but Anne still counted her as her best friend.

Anne walked on the porch just in time to hear Esther's screams.

"Oh my," she thought as she walked into the house to help her best friend give birth to her first child. And as each child came, Anne was there with her. Esther might have been younger than Anne, but she had never had a better friend or a stronger one!

CHAPTER 4
1940

"Oh my sweet Lord!" Esther muttered as she decided to go after the children when her shouting did not work. The wind had gotten so loud that they simply could not hear her.

"Lord, help us…this looks so bad" she prayed as she gathered the children. Esther had never seen a cloud like this before. And she had seen plenty of cyclones in her years.

"Momma, I'm scared!" Ruby Kay whimpered.

"Dear Ruby Kay, it will be okay. We need to hurry and get to the cellar."

"Ah, Momma, why can't we stay outside and watch the clouds? Pa would have let us watch until the rain started and then he would let us run down in the cellar." Joseph always tried to act older than he really was.....

"Children, we don't have time to talk about it, let's get down in the cellar," Esther shouted over the wind.

"Ma.....Wufus?" cried little Annie as she clung to Esther's arm. "Wufus!" Before Esther knew it, Joseph had taken off to get the dog. Rufus was barking at the wind as if his barks would protect his family.

"JOSEPH!" Esther shouted as loudly as she could. She had to get the children in the cellar, but now Joseph was headed in the other direction.

Esther put Little Annie and Ruby Kay's hands together and pointed down the stairs. "GO NOW!" she yelled as Ruby Kay's trembling lips gave away her fear.

"Yes, Ma'am" she mouthed. Little Annie was wailing now. "Wufus, Wufus!"

Esther braced herself against the wind. This was not a regular cyclone. The wind would whip one way, then the next second go the opposite direction. It reminded her of a book she had read about a hurricane near the ocean when she was in school.

Joseph soon ran up to Esther carrying Rufus.

"HURRY SON!" Esther grabbed Joseph's arm and pushed him down into the cellar.

"Wufus" cried Little Annie as she buried her face in his fur. Joseph and Esther pulled the door closed.

"And not a minute too soon," thought Esther as the freight train roared. The crashes soon began. It sounded like their house was falling in on top of them!

This storm was different from any Esther had ever heard. Usually, cyclones stopped as quickly as they started. This one seemed to go on and on.

"Momma" whispered little Annie as her tiny lips quivered. "Stop it pease."

"Oh I know sweetie, I know…please Lord. Let's just pray."

"Where's Uncle Oscar and Aunt Anne?" Ruby Kay asked timidly. Both girls were crying. Esther was almost in tears herself. Would it ever stop? Were their friends ok?

"It'll be okay," Joseph responded loudly over the roaring of the wind. "It'll be okay."

Esther knew that he was trying to convince himself as much as he was trying to convince his little sisters. He took the responsibility of being the "man of the house" very seriously since William had passed away.

"Thud!" The cellar shuddered violently. It sounded like the big old oak tree fell in on the house.

"Momma!" little Annie cried. Ruby Kay sat very still, but her eyes revealed her fear. The girls were crying, Joseph was trying not to cry and Esther was praying.

The storm seemed to go on for hours. It actually lasted around ten minutes, but it was not a normal. The silence was deafening once the wind quit blowing.

"Momma, we have to see what has happened to the house," Joseph said with the authority a grown man would carry. Esther knew that she and the children had to climb the stairs to get out of the cellar and see the damage.

While the girls whimpered, Joseph forged ahead and pushed on the cellar door. His small body could not do much, but he knew something was blocking the door and that it had to be moved.

"Come on Joseph, let me get next to you and I will help you push," Esther said as she climbed the stairs to the door. "Come on son, we can do this," Esther said hopefully.

Each pushed with all their might, but Esther knew how difficult it would be with just her strength plus her little boy's. But thankfully, the table that obviously slid onto the door had now somehow slid off.

The young family walked up shielding their eyes. They saw the sunlight, but it was not coming from the window. As Esther suspected, that old giant oak tree had fallen through the kitchen roof and somehow slid off the roof to the side of the house.

"How did that happen?" thought Esther. "Thank you, God, but what a horrible mess." The girls once again began to cry. "Girls, at least we are safe," Esther said quietly, swallowing her own tears.

Of course, Joseph was the first to volunteer to climb on the roof to check out the damage. "Momma, I can climb on the roof and put the old building wood over all the holes."

"So are you going to patch them big 'ole holes with your bare hands silly?" said Momma.

"Momma, bats? cried little Annie. She was so afraid of the bats she saw flying around at dusk every night.

"Children, I don't know what we will do, but God will help us. He has always been faithful and He will continue to be so."

CHAPTER 5
1940

"Esther, CHILDREN....ARE YOU ALL RIGHT?" yelled Anne and Oscar. Their best friends and neighbors of many years panicked when they saw the holes in the roof and the tree lying on the side of the house.

"WE ARE FINE!" shouted Esther from the kitchen.

Anne and Oscar embraced the family. "Although I wish I could say the same for our roof and house."

Anne assured little Annie that no bats would visit her during her sleep.

"Aunt Anne, I was really scared," mumbled Ruby Kay.

"Ah, I wasn't scared at all," Joseph boasted. Anne and Esther glanced at each other with a small grin.

"Well, Joseph, I did a little shaking and a lot of prayin because I was pert near more scared than I have ever been in my cotton picking life," Oscar interjected.

Oscar had done so much for the family since William had passed. Esther would not have made it if not for the Bell family. She felt like she was taking advantage of them all the time.

"Nonsense," said Anne. "Helping you and the children is a gift to us," she would say over and over.

The Bells had never been able to have children. Already in their 50's, they had all but given up on the idea. They prayed daily and often thought of Sarah and Abraham.

But they truly felt like the time for children was passing them by. Esther and William's children had indeed been a gift to them in so many ways. Aunt Anne and Uncle Oscar had been a provision to Esther and the children as well.

"Our house did not have a bit of damage. Just like those terrible storms, it will hit one house and hop right over the next," said Oscar. "I will get on the roof and see what I can do."

"Well, you be careful up there...just see what needs to be done and I will figure it out." Esther said as she surveyed the yard.

"Uncle Oscar, you know that you cannot go up their alone, so I will help." Oscar hesitated, but Joseph was determined.

"Okay, but son, you will have to be careful. I know that we are a team." Soon enough the team was down.

"Well, we need to go to town to get something to patch those holes. But honestly, we are going to have to find someone real soon to replace that roof so your floor don't rot. It doesn't look like we are to get more rain, so once it is patched it will hold for a little while," said Oscar.

Anne, Esther, and the girls began to clean up the mess in the kitchen that the holes had left. The girls actually helped even though they were small. They seemed to realize that doing their best was important.

Oscar and Joseph left for town. Oscar secretly hoped they could patch the roof well enough to hold until someone could replace the entire roof. The kitchen was usable and that was all that mattered to Esther right now.

"Esther, Oscar said that this floor may have to be replaced if it doesn't dry out. That mold and mildew can grow mighty fast," Anne said while trying to sweep what she could.

"If so I can hire someone. I still have a bit of money that William left me for emergencies. I just had hoped I could hold on to it for a little bit longer."

"I still cannot help but wonder if he knew he was dying. He had saved up without me even knowing about it." Esther tried to muffle the catch in her throat.

Oscar and Joseph came back with a few things.

"Esther, we will do the best we can with them there holes. It seems like lots of folks had damage. It might take a while to get someone to put that new roof on." Oscar lifted the supplies out of his truck.

"And according to some, the county jail out of Busby County had damage. Rumor is that a mean old convict escaped, but no one knows for sure if that is true.

"Uncle Oscar, Momma will be careful. Sides, I am here to protect all the girls," Joseph swelled with pride.

The morning seemed to come extra early, especially since it took forever for Annie to believe that the bats would not be in the house hiding. But Esther didn't seem to mind. The humidity was now virtually nonexistent and she was thrilled since she needed to start on her homemade pies.

Esther baked pies and did seamstress work to bring in extra money. She knew that the money William had left would be gone very soon. William had even saved money for a stove, refrigerator, and stand-alone mixer...what a difference it made in her baking.

Again, William had provided as if He knew He was going to his heavenly home. "Lord, did you prepare his heart before he left us?" she thought again.

Startling Esther, there was a knock on the door.

"Excuse me ma'am, but I hear you are looking for someone to fix your roof."

Surprised, Esther replied, "Why yes, I am..but how did you hear?"

"Uh, well I am new in town and I heard word at the store this morning. I would gladly take the work."

"Sir, I thank you kindly, but I don't know you or anything about your work," Esther said more timidly than she intended.

"I would be glad to talk to the man of the house, but I understand you are a widow woman."

Esther did not like the tone of the stranger's voice. "Yes, I am..but my brother...Oscar...he is on his way. He will be here very soon."

"Ma'am, I don't think he will be here too soon. I know he was the one I heard talking just a little while ago at the store when he was picking up supplies for his farm. So, why don't you just open your door a little wider so I can come in and show you all the things I can really help you with..."

His disgusting grin frightened Esther. Esther shivered. She heard the girls out in the yard playing and Joseph in the barn. She was afraid to anger the man.

She uttered a prayer as she heard a car pull into the gravel lane behind her. The stranger looked angry but continued to face Esther. He showed Esther the knife he had hidden under his shirt. His eyes warned her of everything she needed to be afraid of.

"Excuse me folks, but we are looking for a runaway convict. Some folks said he might be in this part of the county." The man appeared to be the new county sheriff.

"Are you two aware of any strangers wandering around here the last couple of days? The storm seemed to cause a lot of damage in Busby County and we think in the confusion this prisoner got away."

Esther began to answer, but the stranger's knife told her to be very careful. "Uh, no Sheriff, we haven't seen anyone unusual."

The Sheriff took a few steps toward the porch.

"How about you there...have you seen any strange fellows that seem out of place?" Without any apparent motion, the sheriff was on the man and wrestled him to the ground. The knife fell away from the stranger and in a split second the man was in cuffs.

Esther let out a gasp.."How did you know Sheriff?" The Sheriff lifted the man up from the ground.

"Well, when he wouldn't turn around and speak to me, I figured he was up to no good. Any man that would allow his lovely wife to do the talking for him had to be plum silly or trying to hide something."

The Sheriff started to place the convict in the back of his squad car. "Looks like you had some storm damage too," he said.

Esther sighed, "Yes, but hopefully I will find someone who needs a job and can put on a new roof."

The Sheriff shut the door as he finished putting the convict in the back seat of his squad car.

"Just be sure it is someone you know and trust."

"Thank you, Sheriff, thank you so much. No telling what would have happened if you had not shown up when you did," whispered Esther.

Thomas tipped his hat. "It's my job ma'am. And please call me Thomas."

"Then I am not ma'am. Please call me Esther." Soon Sheriff Thomas backed down the lane.

Esther found herself staring at the sheriff's car as he left. He had been a hero, he had come out of nowhere.

"Thank you God," she whispered.

"Oh no, my pies! Esther smelled that familiar scent of baking dough and cherries.

After completing seven pies, Esther heard the children come running up on the porch from a sunny morning of chores and play.

"We're hungry Momma," yelled Ruby Kay. Esther was so thankful that they had been protected from even the knowledge of what had taken place earlier. They had been through so much already in their precious young lives.

"Sure," Esther replied "come and get it."

The lunch dishes were done and the kitchen was cleaned, and in spite of the damage, it did not look half bad. Oscar, with the help of Joseph, had patched the roof, but one decent rain would change all that. It had to be repaired soon.

She sat at her kitchen table trying to think of someone who could fix the roof. With limited funds, no one came to mind as she asked the Father for help.

"You have always been faithful Lord, don't fail me now," she said aloud.

Soon there was a knock at the door. Esther stiffened a bit but soon realized that the face looked familiar.

"Why Sheriff Thomas! What on earth are you doing here?" Esther smiled as she extended her hand for him to come in.

"Now I told you to call me Thomas," he answered with a grin. "I am actually off duty and I figured that you need-ed someone that you knew to fix that roof of yours…and I am applying for the job!"

"You want to fix my roof?"

"Yes, I do handy work on the side and the extra money helps me."

"Well, I guess I do know you…" Esther smiled.

And with that…it began.

CHAPTER 6
1907

Oscar and Anne loved each other deeply. In fact, with each passing year, they fell more and more in love if that were possible. They did not remember a time when they did not love one another.

In fact, their families had been dear friends and they grew up together. They played in the late evening after dinner and chores every single night, unless one of them was sick or gone with the family.

"That is mine!" yelled Oscar one day when Anne grabbed his apple.

"No, it is not! I picked it and I am eating it."

"But it was on my Pa's tree." Arguments like this were common for several years.

"My fish is bigger than your fish," Anne commented one Saturday afternoon as they walked home from the pond.

"Is not....you tell fish tales, that is what my Pa says about you."

For some reason, that comment bothered Anne this time. "Fine, let's compare."

They laid their fish in the grass and measured. Oscar's hand brushed Anne's and she blushed.

"What was that all about?" she thought to herself. She had never felt that way around Oscar. Anne's fish was indeed larger than Oscar's, but for some reason, it did not seem to bother him like usual.

"What is wrong with him?" Anne thought, "He is not even arguing with me about it!"

"Let's lay down in the grass and watch the clouds," Oscar suggested. Soon they were laying next to each other pointing out the dog and beaver. They giggled and laughed.

Oscar wanted to know why Anne thought one cloud looked like a dog and one a beaver. He wanted to know as much as he could about Anne's thoughts.

This was very strange. "Why do I care what Anne thinks?" Oscar thought to himself. He couldn't believe how pretty his best friend had become to him. "What is wrong with me?"

Once they got home, Anne told Oscar good night and felt a slight flutter in her stomach. Oscar felt it too. Anne laid in bed that night with the breeze coming in the window and could think of nothing but Oscar and that feeling. What was happening to her?

Not too far away, Oscar was having trouble sleeping too. Anne was his best friend. "What is going on?" he thought. He counted sheep, cows, even fish! Nothing helped him sleep…until he thought of kissing Anne….over and over.

Things were never the same between them after that day of fishing.

"How many children do you want to have Anne?" Oscar asked one night as they sat on the swing of her parent's porch.

"I want as many young ones as possible," Anne replied with a grin on her face.

"Now why on earth would you ask me such a personal question kind sir?"

Soon Oscar was off the swing and down on one knee.

"Darlin, I have talked to your Pa and he gave his blessing….will you see fit to become my wife?"

Anne began to cry. "Oh Oscar, I would be so happy to become your wife...and fill our home with a bunch of little Oscars!"

"And little Annes," he said as he kissed her with more passion and love than he thought possible.

No one was surprised when the couple announced their engagement at a church social that Saturday night. In fact, one of the deacons asked Oscar what had taken him so long?

"Son, I was afraid we were going to have to take you aside and tell you what was obvious to the rest of us!" Mr. Cooper slapped Oscar on the back while the rest of the men laughed.

Oscar wondered why it took him so long to see something that almost everyone else saw right off.

"I guess I am a slow learner Mr. Cooper!" Oscar said with a grin.

Oscar and Anne decided that they would not have a long engagement.

"Let's just run off to Freeman and get married when the Justice of the Peace gets there," Oscar said with a sheepish grin.

"Oscar Earl Bell, we will get married at a church! Don't you dare think about us running away to get married! My Momma would kill me! And you wouldn't be in much better shape with your momma either!"

Anne laughed. Although it sounded wonderful to start their life as soon as possible, Anne knew that honoring their parents was important.

"We will have plenty of time to be married and have a bunch of babies."

The wedding took place on a beautiful spring day. Anne was adorned in a white gown that her mother had meticulously sewn. It was a beautiful high collared, high waisted gown with wide puffy sleeves that would be the talk of the town for years to come.

The church was decorated with the lovely spring flowers that Anne loved so much. Peonies were her favorite and had bloomed rather early that year, thank goodness for the early passing frosts!

"Oh sweet Anne, you are a vision!" said Pa as he took her arm to escort her down the aisle of the small church. Anne, Oscar, and their families were loved and respected in the town and the towns around Harris.

The church was full. "I wonder if President Roosevelt will attend?" whispered one of the ladies of the church to her friend as she fanned herself on the fifth row.

Oscar was a nervous wreck.

"You can leave now," his Pa said as Oscar wiped the sweat from his brow.

"Ah stop it Pa! You aren't helping!"

"Son, you are marrying the gal that the Lord has planned just for you, I would be nervous being in front of all those people too. Just focus on your beautiful bride when she walks down the aisle with her Pa and you will be just fine." *This is your bride, and I am the bridegroom.*

The two little flower girls walked down the aisle as the bridal music started. Oscar and the preacher stood at the front of the church waiting. Anne and her Pa stood at the door.

Oscar locked eyes with Anne and tears began streaming down his face. Anne was so in love with this man. Once the ceremony started, everyone had tears....including the pastor!

31

The wedding was one of the most beautiful that the town of Harrison had ever seen. It wasn't that it was fancy, or that the food afterward on the grounds was some of the best food ever eaten by several townsfolk.

No, it was watching two people who were so in love, so meant for each other, so designed by God to be together... become one, Mr. and Mrs. Oscar Bell.

The love present was precious and real. Everyone left with a soft spot in their heart that sweet spring day.

CHAPTER 7
1907

Oscar and Anne were able to move right into the house on his father's property. It had been his parent's first home and they had kept it up for hunting and fishing. Oscar and Anne had worked hard to update the little house and it was perfect.

"Anne, we already have an extra bedroom, so we can start filling this place with children right away!" Oscar commented as he kissed his wife.

"Oscar, we will just wait and see what happens, we have plenty of time!" was her constant reply.

Three months passed by and Anne was not expecting yet. "Oscar, for goodness sake, it has only been three months!"

"I know, I guess I just can't wait to have a little one running around, especially if she looks like you!."

"Me? Well I swear Oscar Earl Bell, I figured a boy would be the first child you would want," said Anne as she kissed her husband on the cheek.

"Honey, as many as we will have, I don't care which one comes first as long as it is as healthy as can be!" Oscar grinned. Just thinking about being a daddy made his heart swell.

Oscar and Anne celebrated their one year anniversary, and no children had come into their lives.

"Oscar, the good Lord will bless us with babies when it is time...he knows the perfect time! One year married is not long and probably good for us." Anne would say over and over again.

Five years, ten years, fifteen years passed. The Lord had not blessed them yet.

"Anne, I don't understand. We live our life according to the Lord. We follow His guidance, we give money to the church, we help feed the widows and the orphans. We do everything we can to please Him. Why can't we have children?" Oscar was simply heartbroken.

"Oscar, I don't know what is going on. But I know that God has not left nor forsaken us. There will be a time for children...if there is to be a time for children"

"To think that the Lord is not 'blessing us' because we don't have children is just hurtful. I hate hearing people whisper about it around town.

"And I also don't think just because we do all these good things means we should get everything we think we deserve!" Anne was crying now.

"Oh honey, I did not mean to make you cry." Oscar said as he hugged his wife.

"Oscar, I just believe a little differently than I use to about the Lord. I don't know why we don't have children, but I do know one thing. It is not because the Lord does not love us, or trust us. It is not because of anything we have or have not done."

"I have learned through this past fifteen years that I trust Him. I trust Him with my life and whether or not we have any children on this earth is okay. I will never say God has 'blessed' me if we have children. The Lord has 'blessed' me even if we don't."

Oscar smiled. "My sweet Anne, you are constantly amazing me with your Godly wisdom. The Lord 'blessed' me when He decided you were to be my wife!"

Anne's towel soon was rolled and hit him on the behind.

"Now dear sir, you get out of my kitchen and go take care of the chores outside...you'll think 'blessed.'" Oscar headed outside with a laugh.

"Lord, you know my heart. You know Oscar's heart. We trust you with our lives...with or without children. Help us to be surrendered to you each and every day. Help us to appreciate each other, and help us to be grateful for all we have. I will not take thought for tomorrow, for today has enough going on in it."

"I thank you, Lord, for your love, my salvation, and my precious husband. In Jesus Name I pray, Amen."

For my thoughts are not your thoughts, neither are your ways my way.

Anne smiled and went on and finished the dishes.

CHAPTER 8
1937

The rain was horrible, and there were times he could not even see out of the windshield. But the rain only added to the trip that Thomas thought he would now never complete.

There had been some wonderful experiences as he traveled from Tennessee to New York City, but these last few days made him doubt his decision to leave almost as much as when he was first heading out.

Had his Momma been right at first? Was he being foolish for leaving? No, she had changed her mind, so this had to be right. It was just tough, and he was lonely. *Your decision son.*

It had been rough the last few years at the farm. His father had died in World War I when the ship he was on was torpedoed by the Germans sailing from France in 1918.

Thomas was just a baby then and his older brothers were trying to run the farm. But now they had their own families to care for as well. Things were better now and so he knew it was his time.

The stock market crash in 1929 had upended the country. Thomas and his brothers had heard about it in town while gathering supplies on that Tuesday.

Later that evening while sitting around the radio, they heard more about what had happened. None of them were too familiar with the stock market, but they knew it was bad.

Each year things got worse. They did not get top dollar for their crops or cattle. The banks were closing, people were leaving town. People were losing their farms.

Somehow Thomas and his family were able to hold on to theirs. Maybe it was because their momma would not allow the banks to keep her savings.

Actually, it was something Thomas' momma "felt in her spirit".

"Boys, you all can complain and fuss all you want. I am not taking our hard earned money and putting it in no bank. Why would we take all that money to a building just to have to go back to it and get it out again when we needed it? That is plum silly. I won't do it."

"Sides, the good Lord has put something in my soul say'n I am to keep it here with us," Fannie said with firmness in her voice. She then filled the metal box with the money and buried it in the yard.

She would save the money under the bed and when she got the exact amount she wanted, she would dig up the box, add the money and find another spot. It really looked like the dog had not been able to decide where to bury all his bones.

Thankfully, his mother had listened to that still small voice. She was able to dig up the money when they needed it, while their neighbors lost their money because it was in a bank and the banks closed.

"Yes, Momma, you did the right thing. I am glad you listened to that voice." Thomas did not tell her that the money would not last forever.

His brothers were trying to keep their places going but ended up moving in the old family farmhouse so they could all work together.

There were a lot of mouths to feed, but it was good to have family side by side. And since they were together and combining resources, they were able to help the folks in town who did not have anything except the clothes on their backs.

Thomas and his brothers were talking one evening after everyone had gone on to bed. The radio was off and Thomas felt it was time to talk, time to let his brothers in on what was going on.

"The floods have been awful in this area," Seth said to his brothers. "Even though our fields are not as bad as some, it is going to take a lot of time for them to dry out. Some folks are say'n we got over 21 inches of rain!"

"It is like nothing I have ever seen, " replied Andrew. "I never remember it raining this much in January."

"And to think there are some years we prayed and prayed for rain," Thomas stated as almost an afterthought.

"We just have to be thankful. I know that other people didn't fare as well, but at least we have been able to help them." Seth said to his brothers.

"I don't understand how that happens. Why doesn't the good Lord protect everyone?" Andrew knew how Seth felt. He had often asked himself the same question.

"I don't know if this is right or not, but seems like I re-member Pa talking about this when we was little."

"He said that when God created this big 'ole world that it was perfect. Then sin came into the world when Adam and Eve messed things up. So now there are bad things that happen. It isn't that God doesn't love us when bad things happen, but that is when we have to depend on Him cause He is always there," responded Andrew.

"I guess that really is true. If you think back on all them passages we learn in church and when we read it says God loves us. Scripture talks about it over and over. And I know when we found out that Pa died on that ship, I could feel God right with me," Seth added.

"I have felt that presence too," said Thomas. "In fact, I think I have felt Him speaking to me a lot lately".

"Boy, are you going to tell us what is going on?" Seth asked as he poured them all another cup of coffee. "You always got something in the big 'ole head of yours, Thomas."

"Out with it," Andrew grinned.

"I have had this on my mind for the last few years, but pushed it out."

He was nervous. His brothers had been on him about courting and starting a family. Their wives were even worse. They were always fixing him up with all the new girls that came to town.

Seth yelled, "You getting married? I knew that gal Mary would finally get you hitched."

"Uh-no! She ain't my type," Thomas snickered.

"Then it is that other new gal that has been visiting her aunt the last couple of months," Andrew laughed.

"Stop! You are going to wake up Momma, and she ain't ready to hear this," Thomas whispered.

"Uh-oh. Okay brother, tell us what has been going on in that thick head of yours!" Andrew draped his arm around his little brother.

"It has not only been my head but in all my thoughts and dreams," Thomas said. They all set back down and Thomas began.

CHAPTER 9
1937

"I know that the last few years have been hard, and like I said, I did not want to talk about it. But it seems like things are getting better all over the country, at least that is what President Roosevelt says on the radio," Thomas began.

"I think that is true. But around here folks are hurting from the flood, so I don't know if I would say that too loud," Seth took another drink of coffee.

"Well the good news is at least the President is able to help out the valleys and all the towns and counties around the rivers," Andrew added.

Thomas cleared his throat. "I think it is time for me to leave. Momma is doing well, you two and your families are here and the farm is okay."

Andrew began to twirl his hair around his finger. He did that whenever he was deep in thought.

Seth just sighed. "You have never said that before Thomas, I don't understand, I thought you loved the farm?"

"I do love the farm. More than anything, but I really feel the Lord is pulling me. Don't know why, but I have to venture out," Thomas said with passion.

"Mercy, you sound just like momma," said Andrew. Just as they did when Thomas was born, and several times since then, the two older brothers surrounded him with their arms and their prayers.

The dawn seemed to come a little earlier than usual the next morning. Thomas woke and walked into the kitchen with a bit of dread.

"What if she doesn't support me or understand?" he had asked his brothers before they turned in last night.

"Ah, you know Momma, she will cry a bit, question you a lot, then pray for you as you go. She has never wanted to stand in the way of the Lord in any of our lives. She always worried we were staying here just because Pa was gone. She will be okay Thomas, trust God in this," Andrew assured him.

You know that for those who love me, all things work together for good, for those who are called according to my purpose. When Thomas thought of verses like this, he knew it was time to talk.

"Good morning dear Momma, don't you look especially pretty this mornin." Thomas was grinning with that mischievous smile when he had an idea.

"Oh how I wish his Pa could have known him," thought Fannie.

"Sit down son, if you want to talk we've got some time right now. Your brothers have already gone out, so things are gettin' done. What is on your mind?" Fannie said with a bit of fear. *Fear is the opposite of faith.*

"Momma, you know that I love you and I love Andrew, Seth, the girls, and all the kids. You know I love this farm and have worked really hard at least the last 15 years." Thomas' words rushed out of his mouth like the roaring Mississippi River.

"Son, son, slow down. You sound like one them big 'ole rivers around here. Take a breath and tell me what is going on," Fannie said.

"It is time for me to leave the farm." There he said it. Then why was his heart beating so fast? His momma had always told him to follow the Lord when He felt Him speaking. And he thought He had been speaking for a very long time. He knew he would not be alone.

"Leave the farm?" Momma questioned quietly with a slight catch in her throat. "You want to get a place on your own. Son, are you getting married to Mary finally?"

"No Momma!" Thomas yelled with more intensity that he had intended. "No, Momma I am sorry, but I am not marrying Mary. I don't know who I am suppose to marry, I just know that I have not met her yet." Thomas' tone was softer now.

"So you want to buy one of the farms that are need in' some work in the area?"

"Momma, listen...I am going to New York City." Thomas' voice was very calm now.

"New York City?" was all Fannie could say before she began to cry into her handkerchief.

This was not going as Thomas had hoped it would go. But he was her baby and the last boy. Thomas was old enough and ready to get out into the world.

All he had ever known was farming and it was time to follow a different path. He had to do it before he was tied down with a family.

He had never been able to even consider college, and he had a real interest in the textile industry. He had read all about New York and he knew it would be like nothing he had experienced before.

He was leaving, whether his momma understood or not. He had just hoped she would. Thomas tried to talk to Fannie again, but she simply could not stop crying and murmuring "New York City" over and over again.

She acted like her heart was literally being broken in two pieces. He sat his cup down and decided to go on out to the fields with his brothers.

Thomas went out the door and into the barn where Seth was sharpening some blades. "So, how did it go?" he asked timidly.

"How do you think it went? She is none too happy, and all she could do was sit down and cry while saying 'New York City' over and over. Like it was the worst place in the world." Thomas was so frustrated. "Like it is hell or something!"

Seth listened and continued sharpening the tools. "Give her some time Thomas, she will come around. She thinks it is close to hell I reckon. You know how Momma is…she will think about it and pray about it and be okay with it soon."

"That's just it Seth, I am not waiting around forever for her to get used to it. I am leaving as soon as possible."

Andrew walked into the barn and heard Thomas' remark. "So, it did not go so well with Momma, huh?"

"No, she is going to be unreasonable about this and she can't keep me here!"

"Brother, if it is indeed something you are to do, don't you think God will make it all right with Momma?"

"I am not waiting on that, I want to leave soon. There are things I want to see and do. Her emotions are too tender to even hear from God right now,"

"Hmmm, well you do have that right to make your own choice little brother. Just remember that God does let us make our own choices, right or wrong," Andrew became a little concerned with Thomas' attitude.

Seth and Andrew looked at one another. Soon they were all back to work and not another word was said.

CHAPTER 10
1937

When Mary heard that Thomas was leaving Masonville she was sick. "How can he possibly leave a place that he had called home all his life? What on earth am I going to do?" Mary cried as she walked home from school with her best friend.

"Oh for goodness sake Mary, Thomas barely knows you exist, why in the sam hill do you think he should stay?" Bessie cried.

"His momma is the one who is sick. Why my momma told me that Miss Fannie can't even bear the thought. She won't talk about it to any of her friends, and won't even ask for prayer for Thomas and his trip. It is like she is pretending he isn't going!" Bessie shared.

"I think I will pretend like he isn't either," cried Mary.

"Oh my word, I give up!" Bessie left and took the lane on to her house.

Fannie did everything she had to do outside for several days without saying a word to the boys. She went about her normal routine and in the afternoon, rather than sit on the porch and drink her sweet tea, she would go up to her bedroom.

She decided that she needed to read the good book and pray. The problem was, she did not want to pray because she knew what the Father would say.

One afternoon she could be heard pleading with God.

"Oh Father, I love all my boys, daughters and grand-kids. And I hate to admit it, but sometimes I think I love that baby boy more than any. Lord, that ain't right of me, so I already ask for forgiveness. It is just that after Alfred

died...well, Thomas being born was something special from you."

"He looks like his pa, acts like his pa and has the same sweet spirit. And yes, he is stubborn. Oh, I know that is not from his pa, I know...I know. I just need your peace Lord to get through him leaving me."

As Fannie opened her Bible to the next set of verses, she read "Can a woman forget her suckling child, that she should not have compassion on the son of her womb? Yea, they may forget, yet will I not forget thee." from Isaiah 49:15.

Fannie just cried. "Okay Lord, okay....I will put aside my selfish thoughts and encourage my boy. I know that you be never leave his side. But....I will need help," Fannie whispered.

She closed her Bible and went down to fix supper. She had some things to discuss with the family, and she would not delay a moment longer.

Thomas had agonized for two days about his momma's attitude. He could not believe she was being so stubborn about it! Why was she like that? He had been a good boy all his life, never really giving her a moment's trouble. Oh, he did the normal boy things, but evidently, compared to Andrew and Seth he was a saint.

Why did Momma not remember that? "Lord, I need your help. I cannot change Momma's mind...only you can. And if you don't change hers, I do not want to go all the way to New York without her feeling good about it. But I will do it." Thomas murmured.

Fannie put supper on the table with the help of her wonderful daughters-in-law. She was so grateful to have some women in the house.

When the boys married the girls, she was not really good at knowing how to talk to them since she had raised only boys. But they were patient with her after a few misunderstandings and she was as close to them as she would have been if they had been her very own flesh and blood.

And when Seth and his wife had her first grand baby, Fannie could not have been happier. And it was a little girl. Fannie had so wished Alfred was around to have a baby granddaughter. She would have wrapped her PaPa around her little finger.

"Momma, this looks like a feast, are we celebrating something?" asked Marie.

"You could say that," Fannie replied.

"Looks wonderful Momma, you have outdone yourself," said Nicole. Nicole went out and rang the bell on the porch. The "come and get it" bell had been used for years, and it still did its job.

Seth and Andrew ruffled Thomas' hair as they started for the house.

"Thomas, get rid of the long face, it is really getting hard to keep lookin at that ugly mug all the time!" Seth punched him in the arm and took off running.

Soon all three boys were racing to the house like they did back when Thomas just tried to keep up with his older brothers. But this time, he beat them hands down.

"What's the matter old men, can't you keep up with me anymore?" Thomas laughed as he opened the screen door.

"You boys wash up and come on and sit down. We have some things to discuss," said Fannie. They each looked at each other with dread. They knew that serious talk was about to take place. Thomas looked defeated.

Everyone sat down and Andrew gave grace. Soon the food was being passed around and everyone was talking and enjoying the fine meal that Fannie had prepared.

"Lord have mercy Momma, this tastes as good as it looks! What is going on? Even an apple pie?" Andrew was a bit confused.

"I have some things to say," Fannie said.

Suddenly everyone at the table became very quiet. Fannie was a strong, independent woman and had been that way for a very long time. When Alfred died, her determination and will had gotten even stronger.

Everyone in town knew not to cross Fannie. Yet, everyone also knew she was an honest, hardworking, God-fearing woman. She was well respected in town, in fact in the entire county.

"I have been doing some heavy duty praying and reading from the Word," said Fannie.

"And cryin," added Seth.

"Yes sir, I have done that too. I know that I am stubborn, and it takes me a while sometimes to slow down and hear from the Lord, but I do believe I have," Fannie said with reverence.

By then a sewing needle could have dropped and been heard at the table. Even the baby got quiet.

"Momma," Thomas began.

"Now hush boy, and listen to me. I think that if you feel you should, then go on to New York City. It is time you went out on your own. The Lord will be right there with you. He loves you a whole lot more than me if that is possible, and I am saying right here and now that you have my prayers as you go." Fannie wiped the tear slipping down her cheek and took a drink of tea.

Everyone sat in shock. Everyone but Thomas.

47

"Momma, I knew that if I was to go you would know too. I trust God with my life and I also trust you and your judgement. And I had decided that whatever you thought... I would try and follow," Thomas said.

Andrew and Seth looked at one another. That was not what Thomas had told them earlier. But it did make their Momma feel better.

"Well, in that case, I take it all back," Fannie laughed as she began to cut into the apple pie.

.

CHAPTER 11
1937

February could not come soon enough for Thomas. Things were slower on the farm before the planting season, the fields were drying out pretty well. The boys had already thought of a young man they could hire.

"He will do better than all of us combined," Andrew laughed one afternoon as they all finished up the chores for the night and walked to the barn.

"He is a lot younger than us Andrew," Seth replied.

Thomas just laughed. "Gosh, I am going to miss my brothers," he thought to himself as he watched them carry on.

The girls had all been working in the barn all afternoon. The dance was going to be in the barn and they did not want the men messing it up. Thomas had not wanted a party given in his honor, but his family insisted on it.

"Thomas, we may not see you for a while, and we want to celebrate," Marie said.

"That's right young man, you listen to us! You need to talk to everyone that comes out tonight and be polite," Nicole advised.

"Yes ma'am," he said. "Ok yes ma'ams," he repeated.

The more he thought about leaving his family, the harder it was to think about. "What on earth am I doing Lord? Everyone who I hold dear in my heart is right here. What am I doing?"

"Now you men get in the house and clean up. You all look a sight and the folks will be here soon. We have been cooking all day and everyone will be bringing their dishes

too. We will need you to help us set it all up. Now git!"
Fannie yelled.

It seemed like the whole town of Masonville, Tennessee had turned out for the party. The county sheriff even showed up. He lived in the town next to Masonville.

Sheriff Oliver Tipton had been close to Thomas ever since he could remember. He had served with Thomas' father, Alfred, in the war and escaped the torpedoing of the ship that killed his friends.

He was not on that ship because he had come home for his own father's funeral. Sheriff Oliver had a bad case of guilt. He was the only one of his buddies to survive.

Oliver had come around when he got out of the Navy. He took a sheriff job in Ridgely, a town close to Masonville. He married and had his own children, but he never forgot his best friend's boys or widow.

He made sure Thomas learned to fish and hunt and all the other things little boys needed to learn. Thomas loved listening to Sheriff Oliver and his stories. In fact, Thomas had thought at one time he wanted to be a sheriff, but had put that idea on the back burner.

"Thomas, boy, what are you doing leaving us all here to go to that big 'ole city where you won't know a soul?" Oliver asked as he gave Thomas a big bear hug.

"Ah, Uncle Oliver, you know that I have to do this. I have to find out who I am and who I am supposed to be. The good Lord just seems to be pushing me out the door."

"Son, the miracle here is not that you are being pushed out the door, it is that your Momma is allowing you to walk out that door," Oliver explained with a grin.

The night was wonderful There were all kinds of food and plenty of dancing in the barn. Thomas even danced with Mary and a couple of the other girls, much to his dismay.

His sisters had insisted he be polite and kind and when they did not have a partner. Marie pushed him over to the girls.

"Don't go gettin any ideas Marie," he said as he walked toward their corner.

After a few rounds on the barn's dirt dance floor, the fiddle players stopped. Soon everyone was quiet.

Andrew was the first to speak, being the eldest son. "Thank you all for comin to our party for this youngster." Thomas grinned.

"He will always be our little brother, but we are so proud of him. His courage and his willingness to go where the Lord might be guiding is an inspiration to all of us," Thomas thought he saw something glistening in his brothers' eyes and that rarely happened.

Soon Seth was speaking. "We love our little brother, and even though we have always been much older, he always kept up with us and worked as hard as he could. We are going to really miss him and all them muscles." Seth slapped Thomas on the back.

Fannie was weeping, but Thomas knew she would have to say something. He knew his mother well.

Sure enough, Fannie began to speak while choking back all of her pent-up emotion. "Friends and family, thank you all for coming to our little get together. You all have been with us for years."

"We have been through many hard times together. We have helped each other raise barns and raise our young'uns. We have walked through flood waters, survived droughts and years aplenty. We have even made it through the awful depression by helping each other."

"We made it through the death of loved ones…" Fannie paused as she thought of her sweet Alfred. Thomas put his arm around her.

"And we have wished our younger people well when they chose to leave our sweet little town. I guess there is a bit of all of us that goes with them when they leave. They take with them our love and prayers, and my sweet Thomas," Fannie said as she looked into her youngest son's eyes, "You take my heart."

There was not a dry eye in the barn. Andrew and Seth's tears were obvious now.

"Good Lord folks, he is still among the living!" Seth exclaimed. Everyone dried their eyes and had a good chuckle.

"Anyways, we have something to give our sweet little brother."

Thomas could not begin to think about what they had for him. In fact, he was a little concerned since his brothers loved to tease him so much.

Fannie grabbed Thomas' hands and placed a set of keys in them.

"Son, we decided that we wanted you to use the money you have saved up all these years to set yourself up in New York City. So, everyone in town donated some money so that we could fix up that old Ford pickup. Son, it is yours to drive."

Thomas could not believe what he was hearing. He was going to be able to drive himself to the city.

"Brother, this pickup is pert near brand new. Now you can stop when you want to, plus have a truck of your own in that big 'ole city." Andrew said.

"And when you need to sleep and eat you can stop too," Fannie added.

"At least you ain't headed to that old dust bowl in California," yelled one of his friends.

"He does have a little bit of common sense," Seth chuckled.

"He will probably be one of those fancy men in one of them tall buildings and then he will be too good to speak to us," Andrew said as he rolled his eyes.

Thomas grabbed his family and held them in the tightest bearhug ever. Sheriff Oliver was blubbering as he spoke to Thomas, "I love you boy. Take good care of yourself."

"Let's go look at that pickup," the men said as people began to dance and eat again.

"I can't believe this. It looks brand new," Thomas simply stared. "When did you all do this? And how did you keep it from me?"

"That part was easy, you never pay attention to nothing brother," Seth teased.

"Everyone who could work on it did. Even Momma shined up the hubcaps and cleaned the inside," Andrew pointed to the shiny hubcaps.

"I truly can't believe it," Thomas just shook his head as he looked the car over.

People finished up eating the rest of the food and danced a little more before heading off to their homes. Thomas was simply in shock. He was so appreciative that his family had supported him.

He was especially thrilled with his Momma's change of heart. "Only the Lord can change hearts, only you Lord," he thought as he walked into his bedroom for what might be the last time ever.

In two short days, he would be headed northeast. He wondered what adventures lied ahead.

CHAPTER 12

1937

Thomas was up finishing up his packing before he set out for his last day of chores on the farm, at least for a while. He now could take more since he was taking the pick up.

He still thought he was dreaming last night as he glanced out his window. "The truck is there," he thought to himself. It sat near the house looking like a shiny new penny.

"Boy, do you know which route you will be traveling?" Sheriff Oliver surprised Thomas with a visit.

"What are you doing here?" Thomas asked as he spread around the hay in the barn.

"Son, I just had to see you one more time, and I we wanted to give you a little something for your trip,"

"Uncle Oliver, you have done enough for me already. I cannot accept anything else from you," Thomas put his arms around Oliver.

"Thomas, I just could not get your daddy off my heart last night. We talked so many times about your brothers, our dreams for our children.

"All of the family talked last night and we really felt we was to help you. We wanted to give you this little bit of money," Uncle Oliver whispered as he handed Thomas an envelope.

"I don't want to take your money."

"I knew you would say that, but we all decided about it. We had been setting aside some money here and there for years."

"You know your Aunt Sandy would not have agreed to this if she did not feel this was of the Lord," he was quite convincing.

"And you have to take this gift because you will be denying us a blessing if you refuse. We trust you boy, and we know that you will use it wisely. There is not a doubt in my mind that your pa would have helped you do this. I feel like this is from him as well."

The two talked for a few more minutes before Uncle Oliver said he had to go. It was so hard telling Thomas good-bye.

"Son, you know that we will be praying for you. Call or write when you can. Even if you call your Momma, be sure she tells us what is going on."

"I know one thing is for sure, when I call Momma, everyone in town will know once the call goes through on that party line!" Uncle Oliver laughed and gave Thomas one last hug.

"That" morning came sooner than Fannie liked. She had pretty well been up all night fixing food for Thomas to take with him that would not spoil.

After she finished that up she tried to go up and go to sleep, but sleep eluded her. It wasn't that she was worried, she was just anxious.

She trusted the Lord God with all her heart, mind and soul. But this was going to be hard. She asked the Lord to provide her with the strength to see Thomas off.

Thomas walked into the kitchen and saw his momma standing at the sink, looking out the window as she always did. "What am I doing?" he thought to himself yet again. But even as he thought that he had an excitement in his spirit like never before..and yes… a little bit of fear.

The truck was packed and Thomas was ready to get on the road. All the family gathered around the table for breakfast.

"You are not leaving this house without a good breakfast," Momma told Thomas. They all ate and talked and enjoyed each other's company.

"Is this like the last supper?" said sweet Lucas, Seth and Nicole's son. Everyone laughed and had a hard time stopping.

Breakfast was over, and the goodbyes began.

"Now son, you go on. The Lord is with you, sitting right next to you in that truck...now go on and get started!" Fannie said as that single tear pooled in her right eye.

She knew if the good bye lasted too long she would never make it. The family had prayed for Thomas one last time. He got in the truck and took off down the lane.

"Here we go!" Thomas could not help but giggle. He had mapped out his route like Uncle Oliver had said and he wanted to drive the whole day before stopping.

What lied ahead? He could not help but wonder who he might meet, and where he might end up. The world was lying wide open for Thomas and he could not be more excited. He decided to shake the fear that seemed to be rearing its ugly head.

The day progressed very well as Thomas stopped once to fill up the gas tank. He decided it was best to save his money and eat what his Momma had packed.

He found a nice little grassy area and pulled off the side of the road to eat. The day was beautiful, the sky was clear and the temperatures were perfect. What an incredible day to start his journey.

Thomas ate his sandwich and was starting on the pound cake his mom was almost famous for when he looked up and saw a beautiful collie staring at him. He looked hungry.

"Come'on boy, you can have a bite," Thomas said quietly.

The dog timidly walked toward Thomas and licked his hand. "There you go buddy," Thomas gave the dog a piece of meat that he had not yet unwrapped.

"Bubba, Bubba!" Thomas heard the frantic cries from two small voices. "Bubba, please come here! Where are you? Bubba!"

Thomas could hear the voices getting closer, but did not want to frighten them. The dog continued to eat even though when he heard the voices he would look up. He must have been without food for a while because even though he looked up, he did not stop eating.

"Bubba?" asked Thomas. His tail began to wag as he continued to eat. "I better let your little ones know that you are okay Bubba," he said as he scratched behind the dog's ears.

Before Thomas could even yell in their direction, the children saw their dog and began to run. Thomas was not really sure where they had come from. He did not see any farms close when he stopped.

"Bubba!" cried the little boy as he ran up to the dog.

Bubba wagged his tail and began to lick the children's faces. "Hello," said Thomas. The children did not seem to notice or care that there was a grown man sitting on the ground next to the road eating and feeding a dog.

"Thanks, Mister," said the girl as she hugged Bubba. "We have been looking for him for days!"

"Where do you two live?" Thomas asked. They both looked at each other without saying anything.

"Um…we live on the farm just over that hill," said the boy.

"Oh, okay. Well if you would like a ride I could take you and save some walking," Thomas was not sure what their response would be. They actually looked like they had been lost as long as Bubba.

"Are you two hungry?" He knew that they looked like they needed to eat. The children looked at each other. Soon the boy nodded slightly as he looked at the girl.

"Here you go, take the rest of this meat that Bubba was not able to finish," Thomas said as he unwrapped two more slices of the beef his momma had wrapped up for his trip. Once the children began to eat he could tell it had been a while.

"Are you two brother and sister?"

"Yes sir, this here is my sister Violet and my name is Charles," he said as he stuffed another piece of meat in his mouth.

"Lookie here..my momma sent me enough apples to bake some pies or share with a bunch of people." Thomas pulled the apples out of his pouch. "And since I don't have an oven, looks like I need to share them."

The children looked at one another again and slowly took the apples.

"What is your name Mister?" said Violet as she chomped down on the crispy apple.

"Thomas"

"Where you headed Thomas?" Charles asked as he finished eating.

"I am on my way to New York City,".

"Isn't that one of those places with big 'ole buildings that is really far away?" Charles asked.

"Yes it is, I am going there and hope to get a job and stay a while."

"Did you live on a farm?"Violet quietly asked.

"Yes, I did Violet. I grew up there. My momma and brothers live there with their families."

"So you did not have to leave?" Charles asked.

"No," said Thomas.

"Then why would you leave?"

These children were very curious and did not seem to understand why Thomas would possibly leave his farm if he did not have to. This made Thomas think about his answer.

"I left because I felt like I was suppose to go and I always know that the Lord will be with me. He loves me, Violet and you too Charles," Thomas said with total tenderness.

"The Lord don't love everyone. He does not love us. If this is love, I don't like it!" Charles almost yelled.

"Charles, Momma said you should not talk like that!" Violet frowned at her older brother.

The children had finished eating and they seemed ready to get on their way. The sun was setting.

"Just jump in the back of the truck with Bubba and I will take you to your farm. I am going that way anyway," Thomas said with a smile.

"It is a long walk," Violet said. "Mr. Thomas seems nice enough," she whispered to Charles thinking Thomas could not hear them.

Soon all three were in the back of the truck. Thomas did not know what he would find at the farm. But one thing he did know, he was going to get to love on this family. He was glad they had come upon his path.

CHAPTER 13

1937

Thomas drove over two miles. These children were certainly a far distance from their home. What on earth was going on? He knew in his heart there was going to be an opportunity to love on this family.

Charles seemed rather bitter about the Lord and His love. What had caused such a young boy to have such an attitude already in his life?" thought Thomas.

He had seen older folks feeling this way, but never one this young. These children did not seem to believe that the Lord loved them, maybe he would be able to help them see the true love of God.

The farmhouse was visible as he finally got over the hill. Well, at least it looked like it had been a farmhouse at one time.

"Mr. Thomas, you can stop right here and we will walk the rest of the way," Charles yelled into the window as Thomas slowed.

"Nonsense, we have come this far, I will go on to the farm and meet your family." The two looked at each other with dire concern.

Thomas pulled up to the house. The barn and the house were about to fall down. The barn's roof was leaning and their seemed to be rotten boards everywhere.

"What a need," he thought.

"Mr. Thomas, thank you for the ride. You be safe now as you go to the big 'ole city!" Charles, Violet, and Bubba jumped out of the truck and ran into the house. Thomas had been dismissed.

He sat in the truck for a minute. *Take care of the widows and the orphans.* "Okay I will go to the door. I just pray you protect me from being shot in case someone has a shotgun pointed on the other side of that door."

He got out of the truck and went up on the porch. He knocked. No one answered. He thought he heard voices, and he knew the children were in there.

What if they were alone? What if they did not have anybody with them and they were trying to survive on their own? He knew he could not leave until he found out the answers to these questions.

He knocked again and again. Finally, there was a crack in the door as it opened very slowly.

"Mr. Thomas, thanks for letting us off and for the food. But we have to get ready for bed," Charles said as he peeked through the door.

"Charles, I am not leaving until you let me in. I know that something is not right and I can help you," Thomas said with such sincerity that Charles thought about it for a moment, then opened the door.

Thomas was shocked as he walked in, but tried not to show it. The floor was indeed rotted away in some places and dirt was showing through. There were no lights but candles burned in several areas of the home. There was a smell of sickness in the air. Thomas recognized the smell.

Bubba was sniffing around and barking as he looked toward one of the doors in the house. Bubba seemed to recognize the smell as well. He was certainly trying to tell Thomas something.

"Mr. Thomas, we are fine. We can take care of Momma all by ourselves!" Violet whimpered. Charles agreed as he looked nervously toward the door that Bubba was barking at as if to tell Thomas the truth.

"Please let me help you. Take me to meet your Momma," Thomas pleaded. The children looked at each other as they had several times that day and with a slight nod from Charles, Violet led Thomas into the bedroom.

Thomas had to keep from audibly gasping as he saw a very frail woman lying in a bed.

"Hello Ma'am, I am Thomas and have had the honor of meeting your children today." Thomas kneeled down to the woman's bedside.

With all the strength the woman seemed to have, she responded Her voice was frail as well.

"Thank you, kind sir. The children have gone on and on about you and your help. Thank you so much for helping my babies," the lady said. Bubba had followed Thomas and began licking the woman's face.

Charles and Violet began to tell Thomas about their momma. "Momma got sick a while back. She has had to stay in bed for some time now. But we are taking care of her," Charles explained.

"Momma will get better soon Mr. Thomas, we just know it!" Violet laid her small hand on her mother's cheek.

"What is your name Ma'am?"

"Vera" she whispered. "Charles, Violet, you two go on so I can talk to Mr. Thomas. Thank you for taking such good care of me darlings. Bubba, go on with the children."

The three scurried out of the room, although Charles looked pretty protective as he left. Thomas decided to pull up a chair next to her bed.

He waited. He felt like it was important that he give Vera a chance to explain what was going on before he started asking too many questions.

"Mr. Thomas, thank you again for all you did for my children. I am a good mother, I am just down on my luck a bit. But once I am better we will get back on our feet," Vera murmured.

"I have been sick for several weeks now. The children have been staying home to take care of me. My husband passed away over a year ago. He was sick and was not able to keep up the farm," Vera struggled to continue.

"After he passed away, we tried to keep everything going. Then I got sick and I have not been able to do anything." Vera needed to rest from talking.

"Was there no other family close by?" thought Thomas. "How could these folks be left to deal with this all alone? What is going on here?"

As though Vera could read his mind she slowly responded, "We don't have any relatives close by at all. And we really kept to ourselves and did not visit with our neighbors."

"No one knows what is going on. I have kept the children home and schooled them. We needed them on the farm since we were doing all the work ourselves. We were trying to get ahead but did not seem to be able to do it."

Vera again had to rest again. This conversation was wearing her out. Thomas was worried.

"Miss Vera, if I may ask you a couple of questions?" Thomas asked politely.

Vera nodded "yes." "What is wrong with you? Have you seen a doctor?"

Vera's voice was extremely raspy now. "No, I can't afford one and I don't want to send the children into town by themselves. They go out looking for food, but that has not been going well either." Vera was so weary.

Thomas knew Vera was in pain, but she never complained. She was a strong woman, that he could tell.

"What about the town folk, couldn't someone help you from the church?" Thomas asked. "We never got involved in the church. My husband said all they wanted to do was take our money anyway." Vera let a tear slip down her cheek.

Thomas could tell Vera had talked all she could talk today. He knew he had to let her rest.

"Ma'am, if it is okay with you I would like to help a bit. Could I bed down in the barn for the night?" he asked.

Vera nodded her head "yes" again as she closed her eyes and drifted off to sleep.

Thomas felt her head and knew there was a slight fever. He would sleep in the barn and head out to town early tomorrow to fetch the doctor and get some food.

"Widows and orphans Lord? Help me to help them."

CHAPTER 14
1937

Thomas got up with the sun the next morning. He hoped the day would turn out as beautiful as the sunrise had been. There was always something to be said about a new day. *My mercies are new every morning.*

He knew that he needed to get to town to fetch the doctor for Miss Vera as soon as possible. Charles was at the door of the barn very soon after the sun came up.

"Mr. Thomas, I think we need to go get the doctor real soon for Momma. I am kinda worried."

"Charles, why don't you go with me to town and you can show me where we need to go and we can grab a few supplies before we come back," Thomas said as he walked toward the house. "Violet and Bubba can stay with your Momma. We shouldn't take long in the truck."

Charles looked down at his feet. With the holes he had in his shoes, Thomas wondered if Charles was wondering how much longer he could wear them. Or was he wondering if anyone else noticed them?

"What's wrong Charles?" Thomas asked. Bubba was soon licking Charles' hand.

"We don't have any money for supplies. That is why we have had to go out every day look'in for food. We don't take no charity, that is what my Pa always said."

"Charles, this here is what we call a loan. I will pay for the supplies and you can pay me back someday." Thomas put his arm around Charles as they headed up the shaky steps. That seemed to satisfy the boy's prideful stand.

"Miss Vera, how are you feeling this morning?" Charles asked as he peered in the door.

"She can't hardly talk, but she whispered a while ago that she felt better. Then she fell back asleep," Violet wiped her Momma's forehead.

These poor children were dealing with so much. Many adults would not be able to handle the pressure that they had already endured in their short lives.

"Violet, your brother and I are going to town to fetch the doctor and some supplies. You stay here with your Momma and Bubba and we will get back as soon as we can."

Thomas looked directly at Violet, knowing what her reaction would be. And sure enough, she looked at her brother, waiting for his nod of approval. Charles was indeed her guardian.

Thomas and Charles hopped in the truck and headed for town. Thomas was not sure what kind of reception he and the young boy would receive, but it had to be done.

"Charles, don't you worry none, the Lord will take care of your Momma and you too." Charles looked down at his shoes again without saying a word. Thomas knew what the boy was thinking. *Trust me, son.*

It did not take long to get to town. It was a busy place, and Thomas could tell he was seen as a stranger in town as people took a second look at him and Charles.

"This is the way to the doctor Mr. Thomas," Charles said as he got out of the truck.

"Then let's head that way, Charles."

Thankfully the doctor had not started his rounds yet and was at the door as they walked in. "Hello sir," Thomas greeted the doctor.

Before Thomas could say another word, Charles began, "My momma needs a doctor and she needs you now," Charles yelled.

"Mr. Thomas is loaning me some money so we can get her seen."

"Now, now young man," said the doctor "Slow down. What seems to be the problem?"

The doctor was more than kind when Thomas related all that he knew. The doctor promised he would head out to Miss Vera's farm as soon as he checked on a lady that was about to have a baby.

"But what if that baby decides to get here and you can't see Momma?" Charles cried.

"Son, this little baby won't be here for a week or two, I promise I will get out to your Momma as soon as I can."

Thomas reassured Charles as they walked out of the doctor's office. "Charles, we will get back before he gets there, and he can tell us what is wrong with your momma. Now let's go to the store and pick up a few things." Charles led him to the store.

Thomas noticed the size of Charles' eyes as he saw all the store had to offer. Thomas picked up some necessary staples that the young boy had probably not seen in a while.

He also picked up some vegetable seeds. He thought he could plant a small garden before he left. That was something that could help and something that the children could care for easily.

As Thomas was paying for the items, a nice elderly lady smiled at Charles.

"My momma is sick and Mr. Thomas is loaning us some money to get some things. I'm paying him back as soon as I can. We don't take no charity," Charles volunteered.

"I see," the lady said as she smiled sweetly at Charles, and then at Thomas.

Thomas was not sure if he should respond or not, so he just nodded and smiled back at the woman.

"Young man, could I have a word with you?" the woman asked. Charles had a look of fear in his eyes.

"Charles, go ahead and take these things out to the truck and I will be there soon," Thomas said with reassurance.

Charles took the supplies and headed to the truck. "Don't tell her we ain't in school," he whispered as he walked out the door.

Thomas looked at him thinking "Boy, you started this conversation!" Now Thomas was not sure what he was about to hear.

"Excuse me, I don't mean to pry. But I have seen that young boy and a smaller girl on the outskirts of town alone before. I don't want to do anything but offer my help. I believe I am to find out what is going on," the lady said with concern.

"My name is Mrs. March and I have lived here for years. I am a member of the local Baptist church," Mrs. March offered.

"Thank you, Lord," thought Thomas as he began to tell Mrs. March the story. How the Lord led him to visit while he was on his way to New York and how he had prayed.

"Glory to God Thomas!" Mrs. March said. "We will help them with anything they need, rest assured. It sounds like they need lots of love!"

Mrs. March touched Thomas arm as he told her how to get to the farm. He felt like he had just had a conversation with his own Momma, or at least a guardian angel!

Thomas arrived at the farm with Charles, who had started to call "Charlie".

"Wow, only my Pa called me that! My momma doesn't even use that name," Charles said rather quietly.

"Is it okay? If not I understand," Thomas said.

"It is ok Thomas. Makes me feel kinda good inside," Charles responded.

Thomas pulled some candy out for him and his sister. He had secretly bought some when he finished talking to Mrs. March. Charles' smile was bigger than he had ever seen and most likely one of the only smiles he had genuinely smiled for several months.

Miss Vera was sitting up in bed and looked so much better. He was glad to see her smile.

"Miss Vera, it is so good to see you sitting up!" Thomas said as he brought in some of the supplies and put them on the counter.

"Momma, you are beautiful," Charles said as he kissed his mom on her forehead. Their relationship reminded Thomas of his love for his own momma.

Violet saw the other piece of candy that Charles was holding. "Yes Violet, this is yours. Mr. Thomas surprised us with it!" Charles said as he handed Violet her piece. She did not look for her nod of permission.

Thomas was making progress. "Mr. Thomas has surprised us with a lot of things," Miss Vera said as she looked through the door at the kitchen counter.

"It's okay Momma, Mr. Thomas knows I will pay him back and that we don't take no charity."

"Charles would not owe anyone anything," Thomas thought to himself.

CHAPTER 15
1937

Thomas was in the barn working to clean it up a bit. He found the rotten wood and replaced it. He had several projects that he felt like he should do before he moved on. But how could he get them all done in a short amount of time?

He could not even begin to think about all the work that needed to be done inside the house! Miss Vera had no income and Thomas could do nothing about that...but pray. *Trust me* .

"What's all that racket?" Thomas put down his tools and looked outside just in time to see some trucks coming down the lane.

One truck contained the doctor that they had spoken to in town. Another contained a gentleman and Mrs. March. The other trucks were full of people. All appeared ready to do some work.

"Hello!" Thomas waved as he walked towards the trucks.

"Hello Thomas, I hope you don't mind, but I made a few phone calls and before I knew it we had a brigade of people to help this lady and her precious children," Mrs. March stated.

"Oh Mrs. March, I was just chatting with the good Lord about how on earth I could possibly help them with all that needed to be done."

"Well son, it appears as it did not take Him long to answer that prayer."

The doctor soon had a diagnosis for Miss Vera. "She has pneumonia, is dehydrated and almost starved. I would dare say all the food that she had she gave to the children. I gave her some penicillin, it is a wonder. If she eats and drinks plenty of fluids, she should regain her strength and be just fine in time."

"But son, if I had not seen her today she would most likely have died in a few days. You showed up for this family just in time," the doctor said as he packed up his bag.

Mrs. March was in the kitchen and it was beginning to look like a real kitchen. Her husband and another man were working on the floor. People were working all over the house.

"Thomas?" Miss Vera asked.

"Yes, Ma'am," Thomas answered as he poked his head in the doorway of her room.

"What on earth is going on out there?"

"Miss Vera these people are here to help you. The Lord knew that you and the children needed some help, and He sent them all."

Vera began to weep. "Oh my, I don't deserve to have prayers answered. I have not lived my life like I should have for Him. I have not been to church in years and I have not taken my babies," Vera was weeping now.

"Miss Vera, you mustn't cry. It will make you feel worse. The Lord is not punishing you. He does not give His grace to us based on what we do or don't do. His love is based on what He did on the cross for us," Thomas said.

Mrs. March appeared at the door when she heard the weeping.

"There, there dear one. God loves you and your children so much. It was not an accident that Thomas ran into the children. It was not an accident that I ran into Thomas in the store. God loves you Miss Vera, and He uses His people to show others His love."

"We are going to help you as long as it takes to get you back on your feet." Mrs. March sat on the chair next to Vera's bed.

Thomas stayed on for five days. Mrs. March assured him that now that the church and townsfolk knew of this sweet family, they would never have a need for anything.

Vera had agreed to put the children in school, several of the men agreed to help with the farm until Vera could decide what she should do with it. They felt if they got it back to working order she could easily sell it. Even Mrs. March offered Vera a job.

Thomas was loading up his truck when the children came out to tell him good-bye.

"Thank you, Mr. Thomas," Violet said as she ran up to Thomas. Not afraid to speak to him without permission from his brother now, she looked like she had grown a foot since he had first met her.

"My pleasure," Thomas replied as he swirled her around in the air.

"Yup, thank you, Mr. Thomas. When you get to that city you need to send me your address so that I can repay you for everything. Me and Violet have kept a list and...."

"I know, I know, you don't take no charity," Thomas messed up Charles' hair. "Buddy, the good Lord loves you and I hope that you see that now."

Charles' eyes teared up as he hugged Thomas. "Yes sir, me, Momma, and Violet talked about that last night. I do believe Mr. Thomas. We even decided that we were goin start going to Mrs. March's church," Charles said.

Thomas smiled as he waved goodbye to the children. Mrs. March had brought Miss Vera out to the porch as well. Her tears said it all. "Thank you Lord for using me,"

Thomas thought as he drove away. *Stay surrendered Thomas.*

CHAPTER 16
1937

The next couple of days were really uneventful, especially when he compared them to the last few days! Thomas simply enjoyed driving, meeting people and spending time with the Lord.

In fact, he had not felt so close to the Lord as he did right now. He had no doubt in his mind that he was indeed following His will. He thought the fear he had was practically gone.

He had come across a few people with needs, and as was Thomas' heart…he gave them some money and talked to them about the Lord. He was actually down to a little less than half of what money he had when he left.

"Lord, give me wisdom," Thomas said as he put the remainder of his money in his wallet. *I am your wisdom, holiness and redemption.*

Thomas could barely see the city skyline with all the rain. But he knew he was close to New York City! As he drove he felt the excitement, but soon that gave way to that bit of fear again!

"What on earth am I doing Lord?" Thomas whispered as he passed several cars on the road. I can hardly see and I cannot believe that I am almost here." He thought of his momma, his brothers and sisters-in-law and what the future held for him. Maybe his momma was right.

"What was that noise?" Thomas thought he heard a horrible crash. He looked in his rearview mirror and saw a sedan smoking and sitting in a very large, deep ditch of water. The rain was relentless.

Without even thinking about it, Thomas turned the truck around and stopped on the side of the road. Others had stopped, but no one seemed to know what to do.

"Quick, help me get down to the car before it fills up with water!" Thomas shouted to the men getting out of their cars.

The man in the car could not get the door open. He was yelling for help as the water began to rise. Thomas knew that timing was important. With the help of the other men, Thomas was able to get down into the ditch.

One of the men had a rope and tied it around Thomas' waist. "I am almost there...hold on!" Thomas yelled as he got closer to the door.

The man was in a panic.

"Sir, sir...listen to me. Calm down, I am going to get you out. Lord, help me!" Thomas yelled and prayed. Thomas pulled on the door. He made eye contact with the man and did not look away.

"Keep your eyes on me and push!" Thomas shouted. After what seemed like hours, but was only a couple of minutes, the door came open. Thomas reached and grabbed the man and quickly wrapped the rope around him.

"Hang on sir, the men up over the ditch are going to pull you up. Don't fight them."

"Thank you, son. Thank you," the shaking man whispered as he climbed up out of the ditch.

Thomas got out of the ditch and immediately went to the man. He was wrapped in a blanket and sitting up.

"Son, thank you. You saved my life. I will never forget you. How can I repay you? What is your name? Where are you from?"

"Sir, no problem. I was just in the right place at the right time," Thomas replied.

"What is your name? How much can I pay you?" stuttered the very wet man.

"I am Thomas Smith sir. And you do not owe me anything. I only did what anyone else would have done given the situation."

"Thomas, I am Morris Gold, and I am not sure just anyone would have done what you did."

Mr. Gold took another look at his car that was partially immersed in the large ditch now. "All this rain filled up that ditch pretty well, I should have been more careful."

"Where are you headed son?" Mr. Gold asked.

"I am headed to New York City sir."

"Do you have family or a job to get to?" Mr. Gold shivered in the cold.

"Neither to be honest. I felt as if I was to come to New York City for some reason, so with my family's blessing I left," Thomas said.

Mr. Gold looked at Thomas with curiosity. "I have never heard such a thing son. But if you say so. I hate to ask anything else of you, but could you give me a ride to the city?"

"Why of course Mr. Gold, but what about your car?" Thomas inquired.

"Not a problem, I will send some of my boys to get it. And I insist that once we get there you come to my home and stay. And I won't take no for an answer Thomas Smith!"

Mr. Gold had given the instructions and Thomas knew better than to argue. He would spend the night and look for work tomorrow morning. He was exhausted and he knew that having somewhere to lay his head tonight was not an accident. He couldn't wait to get out of his wet clothes.

Thomas woke and dressed and walked down the long staircase the next morning. "I thought I was dreaming last night when the hired help took me to that huge room. butI guess not." Thomas could not believe the splendor in which the house was decorated. Where was he?

"Good Morning Thomas!" Mr. Gold greeted Thomas from the head of the very large table.

"Good morning sir." He allowed his eyes to survey the large room until he came upon one of the most beautiful girls he had ever seen in his life.

"Son, this is my daughter, Elenor." Mr. Gold smiled as he saw the young people gaze into each other's eyes.

After Thomas had told Mr. Gold he would be looking for a job, Mr. Gold insisted he come to the textile factory. He owned and operated one of the largest factories in the city. He gave Thomas a job before Thomas even knew what had happened.

"Sir, you don't owe me a thing," Thomas told Mr. Gold "I just did what was right."

"I know that son, but I feel like I will be getting a man with a great work ethic and I am excited to see what can happen," Mr. Gold smiled with extreme satisfaction.

The days seem to fly by while Thomas got used to living in New York City and staying in the Gold's home.

"Just until you get on your feet son," Mr. Gold had told Thomas over and over.

Why did Thomas feel a little fear and a tug at his spirit? "Lord, I know that you have provided this for me and I thank you." Thomas thanked God for His provision. *Careful son.*

Thomas had talked to his momma several times and assured her he was fine. He told her where he was staying, what had happened and who he was working for. He was excited and told her of all that New York City had to offer. He had enjoyed parties, restaurants and mentioned Mr. Gold's daughter, Elenor, several times.

"Thomas, do you think it is proper to continue living with this family? Maybe it is time to get out on your own. Especially the way in which you are talking about this gal, Elenor," said Fannie.

"Momma, you are being silly. I really cannot afford a nice place and Mr. Gold says I can say for as long as I want. The house is so huge that my room is several doors down from Elenor.

This is God's provision," Thomas reminded his Momma. She wasn't too sure of that fact.

Elenor and Thomas were definitely attracted to one another, and Mr. Gold knew it and approved. One night they were sitting at the table and Elenor had already gone up to her room.

"Son, I know you have not asked, but I give you permission to court Elenor. I see the way you two look at one another. I have seen your work and would be pleased for you to see her," Mr. Gold commented as he poured himself another drink.

Thomas grinned as he thought of the prospect of Elenor. She was a beautiful gal, had money and he was becoming accustomed to all this glitz and glamor. *Whatever is pure, holy and just...dwell on these things.* Thomas just ignored that thought.

Thomas took Mr. Gold's offer of a drink and would also take the opportunity that Mr. Gold had just given him with Elenor. He easily ignored the fear this time.

Mr. Gold clinked his glass with Thomas. He was formulating a plan. Maybe this God Thomas spoke of was real after all.

CHAPTER 17
1938

The wedding plans were almost complete. In one short week, Elenor would wed Thomas Smith. Thomas would take over the textile factory and Mr. Gold could not have been more pleased.

He would still be in charge, but Thomas would be his "right hand man." Everything he had planned for his daughter was coming true right before his very eyes.

The minute Thomas had rescued him from his car he felt certain that this could be a man that Elenor could wed. He was perfect for her, and she was perfect for him. He had never had a son.

His wife died while giving birth to Elenor. The enormous responsibility of raising Elenor and making sure she would be taken care of her entire life never left his mind.

Mr. Gold had always given Elenor everything she wanted. Everything! She never worked for a thing, and always had people taking care of her every whim.

Thomas had learned this the hard way. One afternoon she had thrown a glass at him when he opposed a decision she had made about the wedding. This was going to be the "wedding of the decade" and she was going to have it her way.

"Elenor, darling..could we wait a couple of weeks so all my family could get here from Tennessee?" Thomas asked, then pleaded.

"No! I told you months ago when we would have the wedding and there was no reason to change it. We can visit your family after our honeymoon darling," Elenor said as she kissed Thomas. She stomped off before he could present more reasons to wait. She had made up her mind and it would not be discussed again.

Thomas had more interesting experiences in the last year than he had in his entire life. But something wasn't right. He could not put his finger on it. He had heard the little warnings in his head, but again ignored them.

But each time he dismissed them as nerves when things had gotten stressful at work. Sure they attended church services every Sunday, but they simply felt like another social gathering, and Thomas had grown accustomed to it.

"Son, are you sure this is what you should be doing?" said his momma one day as he spoke to her on the phone. "Your brothers and I are worried about you. This seems so sudden, and we hate that we cannot get there for the wedding and to see you and talk to you in person."

"Momma, you sound just like you did when I was getting ready to leave. The only reason you all want to see me in person is to talk me out of this marriage!"

"Did you ever think that this is why I was sent to New York City? You just don't want what is best for me!" Thomas yelled into the phone and hung up the receiver.

Fannie was heartbroken, her son had never hung up the phone or been disrespectful to her like that. She grabbed her side once again and winced silently in pain.

The wedding was indeed the "wedding of the decade. " According to the social section of the papers that came out the following week, there had not been one like it in years.

Thomas and Elenor had taken a lavish honeymoon, paid for by Mr. Gold of course. And as he expected, they did not visit his family in Tennessee.

Thomas had wanted to buy a house of their own, but Mr. Gold and Elenor insisted that the house was too big for just

80

him. And of course, Elenor did not want her daddy to live in the house alone.

They would come back from their honeymoon and live there with Mr. Gold. There would be no discussion, both Mr. Gold and Elenor had made that clear.

Thomas was miserable and had been almost immediately after they got back from their honeymoon. Months had passed and he was so hopeful he would feel differently.

What had he done? He had gotten swept up in all the power and things that having money could give you.

But he had not heard that still small voice in a very long time. Where was the Lord? He missed his family, he missed Tennessee. "Lord I need you!" cried Thomas one evening as he sat alone at the dining room table. *I am here son. I never left, you just quit listening.*

Thomas knew it was time to take charge and speak his mind. He thought that going back to Tennessee with Elenor might be just the thing they needed. He could introduce her to his family and move back to the farm. He knew his momma was aging, and there had been strain every time they spoke on the phone.

His brothers confirmed his fears. Not only was she aging, she was sick. Thomas knew he had to move back home. Elenor needed to go with him.

Elenor had been particularly moody the last several weeks. Thomas knew his wife well, and she was always moody if she did not get her way, but something was wrong.

Surely she wasn't sick too? He knew he had to have a difficult conversation with her, but he had a feeling it would not go well. He could not even imagine telling his father-in-law.

"Elenor, we need to talk," Thomas said one evening after they had gone to bed.

"Yes, darling, we do. Can I go first?" without waiting for a reply she blurted out the news. "Thomas…we are going to have a baby!"

Thomas' expression must have shown his mixed emotions. "A baby? Already?"

Elenor began to cry. "I know this is not what we wanted just yet, but sometimes these things happen. I thought you would be so pleased!"

Thomas tried to calm his wife. He knew that a child was a miracle, but the timing could have not been any worse. He knew he had to tell Elenor what he was planning, but he was not sure what her response would be now that she was expecting.

"Dear, I have talked to my Momma a couple of times and she is not well. We have to go visit her at the farm. I want you to meet all my family before the baby comes." Thomas looked deep into Elenor's eyes.

"Just a visit, right?" she asked as she fell into his arms. "We should go before it gets too uncomfortable to travel," Elenor smiled.

Thomas had no intention of just visiting. He was taking his wife and baby to live on the farm where he grew up. He was even more determined not to raise a child in the environment of the city, or with the baby's grandpa giving the child everything it ever wanted. But he knew he simply could not tell her the truth, even though he knew better.

Thomas called his momma the next morning to share the news of their visit. He thought it best not to tell her about the fact that he wanted to stay. He also decided it would be a wonderful surprise to tell her about the baby once they arrived. His momma was thrilled, and she forgave him of his attitude the last few months.

"Son, you know that I love you unconditionally, I am just glad that the big 'ole city did not rob you from us forever," Fannie said.

Mr. Gold was not so supportive. That evening at dinner he made no effort to hide the fact that he was not pleased. Elenor had not even told him about the baby.

"Daddy, we have some good news to share with you," Elenor said as she pushed her plate away.

"Well, the news that I received this morning was not good at all. I am going to have to replace Thomas while you are gone, and no one will be able to carry on with the necessary work like him!" Mr. Gold never had a problem sharing what was on his mind.

"And why aren't you eating? The last couple of days you have pushed your food away as if you don't ever want to eat again. That is not like you at all. Daughter, what on earth is going on?"

Elenor began to giggle. "Oh Daddy, you are going to be a grandpa!" Mr. Gold's expression was priceless. In fact, Thomas had never seen him speechless either. But it changed quickly.

"So in your delicate condition you should not travel," Mr. Gold demanded.

"Daddy, we are just going for a visit, we will be back before I get too big. I would not dare take a trip that far if it would be dangerous for the baby. I am going to the doctor in the morning for clearance. Don't you worry. We won't stay long."

Thomas could not look at either of them.

CHAPTER 18
1938

The trip actually went better than Thomas ever expected. Elenor did not whine much at all. Maybe pregnancy was good for her. Although they did have to stop several times, and it took three instead of two whole days, it was actually a pleasant trip.

"We are so close to home," Thomas said with an excitement that he had not had in a long time.

Elenor got very quiet. "What if they don't like me?" she whispered.

"Just be your sweet self," Thomas replied even as he prayed. "I hope she is sweeter than that Lord." Thomas turned down the road that would take him the last ten miles to his family farm.

As expected, the family was outside on the porch waiting for him. He had called his brother and told him of their delay. He could not wait to tell his Momma about the baby, but first things first. It was time for everyone to meet Elenor.

As he looked at her, he silently prayed that she would be on her best behavior and not become whiney too soon. But he knew it was inevitable.

She was beautiful and glowing and he hoped everyone fell in love with her. No matter what though, he knew his family would embrace her. He was right.

"Oh come here sweet boy, and bring that precious daughter of mine with you!" Thomas thought it was very odd that his momma did not come running to the car as all the others had...then when he looked upon her face and saw all the weight she had lost, he knew why.

She was horribly sick. He tried not to show his shock and concern.

"Thomas, I will tell you what is going on soon," Andrew whispered in his ear as they all walked on the porch.

"Sweet girl, you are beautiful! I am so glad to finally meet you. I knew you had to be pretty special to snag my Thomas!" Fannie kissed her on the cheek once she stood up from the porch rocker.

"I guess I am second fiddle now," Thomas laughed as he grabbed his momma and hugged her tightly. He quickly stopped when he heard an unexpected, involuntary gasp from her.

Something was terribly wrong with his momma. He knew in his heart that this was not good. How thankful he was that he had finally listened and came home.

He glanced at his wife, who sat there in shock. She had never been treated so kindly by people not wanting anything from her. She still did not understand unconditional love.

Thomas shared the story of Miss Vera, Charlie, and Violet. He went on to tell of all his adventures while traveling to New York City. He shared with his family every single detail it seemed.

It was so easy just to be himself around them. He had missed his family more than he realized. He talked for two hours and did not share anything about Elenor and the wedding. He talked about rescuing Mr. Gold…but that was as far as he went with his story. And Elenor noticed.

"Come on in folks, dinner is on the table. We can keep hearing all about your life Thomas while we eat our fried chicken!" Marie called out.

"Yes, and we want to hear about this grand wedding!" Nicole commented as they all headed into the house.

85

"At least someone wants to talk about it," Elenor murmured to Thomas as she walked past him into the house.

They all sat down to eat and Thomas noticed an extra place setting. "Who are we missing?" Thomas asked.

"At least you did not invite the whole town of Masonville to the homecoming like you did the going away party!" Everyone laughed as they started talking about that party.

"Uncle Oliver is coming to eat with us. Since Aunt Sandy passed away he has been very lonely," said Seth.

"What!? When did that happen?" Thomas was visibly shaken.

"I called and left a message with someone," Andrew replied. "I thought it was strange when you did not call back. I just figured you were busy or something. Then when you said you were coming home, I did think it was strange you didn't say anything."

"No one gave me the message," he said as he glanced at his wife. She put her head down and looked at her plate.

Fannie would not let this celebration become awkward, and as if on cue, Sheriff Oliver knocked on the door.

"Come on in!" yelled a chorus of voices. Elenor actually jumped.

"What is wrong with all of these people?" she thought to herself. "What have I gotten myself into?"

Thomas immediately rose from his chair and gave Uncle Oliver a hug. "I am so sorry about Aunt Sandy! I somehow did not get the message or I would have called you," he said with tears in his eyes.

"Oh son, no worries. I figured you would get a hold of me soon enough. There was nothing you could do or say that would bring her back," Uncle Oliver replied quietly.

Dinner progressed as Elenor poked and pushed around the food on her plate.

"Girl, what is wrong with you? Don't you like fried chicken? What about them biscuits? Everyone loves Momma's biscuits!" Seth joked.

Elenor did not seem to get it. "I would like to be excused. I am very tired from the long drive and I have developed a headache. Could you tell me where the guest room is?"

Everyone looked at each other and grinned a bit.

"Dear, we don't have a guest room, but you can have mine and Nicole's room and we will sleep with the children." The look on Elenor's revealed the shock of not having a guest room.

Nicole got up to take Elenor to the room.

"Come with me Elenor and I will get you all set up to rest." She glanced back at her husband and lifted her eyes.

"This is not going to be easy," Thomas thought as he got up to walk with his wife and Nicole.

"What kind of place have you brought me to Thomas!? Why, there is no guest room! I knew there would not be a maid, but no guest room?"

"Oh my, we will be sleeping is another couple's bed. There is nothing proper or correct about that! We should have gotten a motel room!" Elenor was overcome with indignation.

"Dear, I told you that there was not a motel in Masonville. The motel that we could have stayed in was an hour away," Thomas just sighed.

"Well, you go to that phone and get us a room right this very minute. I will not spend days in this....this....place!"

"Elenor, this is my momma's home and the home in which I grew up. My family lives here. No, it is not as fancy and frilly as the place that you grew up, but it is filled with love and that is something that you obviously know nothing about!"

Thomas stomped out of the room, but not without slamming the door. Thomas would draw the line on her insults about his family, especially his momma!

Thomas headed back to the table to finish the meal and the conversations. "I am sorry. Elenor is just tired from the trip," Thomas offered as a way of an apology.

"Oh son, don't worry about it. Let her rest, she will wake up in better spirits."

"We will save her plate so that when she feels like eating she will have something to eat." Fannie picked up Elenor's plate, covered it and put it away.

"Now you go on with your stories and finish that food. You look like you could put on a few pounds!"

"No Momma," Thomas thought, "you look like that is something you need to do." Why was everyone looking so sad? Something horrible was going on and he knew that it was about his precious momma.

The dinner conversation was so pleasant. How Thomas missed the easy banter he had with his brothers, sisters-in-law and Uncle Oliver. It felt so good to be home.

He hoped that when Elenor decided she was hungry and came out she would have a better attitude, but he had his doubts.

The men headed out for the porch while the women cleaned up. The girls insisted that Momma go out on the porch and visit. But it was obvious that whether she was visiting or not she was not able to help with much of anything.

Thomas took her arm and led her back to the rocker. They all sat quietly on the porch for a few minutes before the girls brought out the pie and coffee.

"Let's all sit together and eat this," Momma motioned to the girls. She was not eating and Thomas knew she had just pushed her food around on her plate at dinner.

Marie and Nicole agreed with momma and went in to get their pie and coffee. Thomas heard Elenor's voice.

"Why yes, we can fix you anything you want. And why don't we all sit here while you eat and finally tell us about that wedding!" Thomas knew that Elenor was dying to talk about it, and it would give him time to find out what was wrong with his momma.

"Your Aunt Sandy just did not get up one mornin." Uncle Oliver said. "She did not complain of anything at all the night before. I knew she was gettin a bit more winded when she would do things in the house, but she just laughed it off saying that he old age was catching up with her." Uncle Oliver truly looked lost.

"I am so sorry, I can't imagine your pain." Thomas placed his hand on top of Oliver's. "She was a fine woman, none finer," Thomas shared.

"Now if we could just get something done for your momma!" Uncle Oliver started the conversation that Thomas had wanted to start.

"Ah, Oliver, hush up. I ain't got nothing to say, you know that," Momma said.

"Momma, it is time to tell Thomas what is going on. He is here in person, so there is no need to hide it." Andrew addressed his mother as Seth nodded.

CHAPTER 19
1938

The boys and Oliver settled down on the porch with their coffee after finishing their pie.

"Okay Momma, either you tell Thomas or I will," Andrew said quietly.

"Okay young man…Thomas, I am going to be with your daddy real soon."

What was Thomas hearing? Had he heard his momma right? He looked at his brothers and at Oliver with questions. They all put their heads down as Fannie continued.

"Son, I have cancer. According to the doctors, it is one that simply cannot be cured. They tried those radiation treatments and they just made me sicker than an old coon dog. It was no way to live and they were not working anyhow."

"Momma, why didn't you tell me?" Thomas' emotions were all over the place. He was mad at his brothers for not telling him as well.

"Why didn't you two tell me about Momma when we talked? You had plenty of opportunities. You could have brought her to New York, those doctors are always trying new treatments." Thomas simply could not believe what he was hearing.

"Thomas, I told your brothers not to tell you. You had enough going on with the wedding and your new job. I was not about to have you upset and coming home when we really did not know what was happening. Then when we found out, it was too late to let you know. At that point, I would not be the cause of your wedding being postponed."

"So that is why you all kept saying you couldn't make the trip at that time!" He understood now.

"But Momma, please...let's go back to New York. Elenor's dad could find us the finest of care. We can get doctors that know what they are doing and can make you well. We have to try!" Thomas then was lost to all the emotions he had carried inside since he married Elenor. He wept in his hands.

Fannie looked at Andrew, Seth, and Oliver. They knew that look meant for the time being they were dismissed to go inside. Fannie needed time with her youngest son. She went over to the chair right next to him.

"Now, now Thomas...it will be all right. I am ready to go home. I am tired. I want to see your Pa. I have missed him so very much and I am ready to see the face of Jesus."

Thomas continued to weep with his head down. "But I am not ready for you to go home, I just finally made it back to mine," Thomas whispered as he lifted his head to hug his Momma.

They sat in silence for a long time before the others joined them again on the porch. This time the girls came and Elenor came with them.

"Oh Thomas, what a lovely wedding you two had...I cannot imagine the size of that cake. Elenor said she had photos packed away, so maybe can see them soon." Marie said.

"Sure, sounds great," Thomas replied with no enthusiasm. Elenor took it quite personally.

"Dear, the wedding was beautiful. You should be proud of it. It was the social event of the season."

Thomas looked at her with the eyes of a man no longer in love with his wife. Had he truly ever been in love with her? Or was he in love with the elegant lifestyle and money?

Of course, Elenor did not appreciate it and before another conversation had started she offered her excuses and good nights and left without even so much as reaching down to tell Fannie good night.

"How rude is that woman!" Thomas thought. She is so self-centered and thinks only of herself.

The night wore on and one by one the porch became empty. All but Oliver and Thomas remained.

"Thomas, I am so sorry you had to hear the news of your Momma like that. I know that you are mighty hurt. Why don't you go on to bed with that sweet bride of yours and let her help you get through this."

"Get through this? She won't be able to help me with anything. She was bad before the pregnancy, but now it was ten times worse," thought Thomas.

Oliver was a bit in shock, "Thomas, Thomas…are you all right son?"

"No, Uncle Oliver, I am not all right, and unfortunately going in and being with my lovely wife won't help one bit."

Thomas took a deep breath and headed in to go to bed. He knew he had to go into the room with his wife or he would never hear the end of it. When really all he wanted to do was curl up into a small ball and sleep in the barn where he always could do his best thinking.

Oliver stayed on the porch praying that the young couple would have what he and his precious Sandy had, knowing it was never too late for the prayer to be answered.

Thomas entered the bedroom of his brother and sister-in-law on his tiptoes. He was not in the mood to have to discuss anything frivolous with his wife. *She is carrying your child.*

He was reminded of how excited he was at the thought of having a child. He knew that Elenor was particularly sensitive, but he was hoping she was sound asleep. Elenor stirred. He stopped dead in his tracks.

"Thomas, what on earth are you doing coming in so late? You know that I hate to go to sleep without you right next to me. It is very important. And this room feels so awful that I needed you in the worse way. You could at least act like you care."

So much for her being asleep. Thomas had no fight left in him tonight. He responded with the words he had said far too many times in their short marriage.

"Yes dear," and he climbed into bed. Soon he could hear her deep breathing. He did not sleep at all.

The next morning Thomas got out of bed and headed straight for the kitchen. Elenor was still asleep, so he welcomed the respite. He entered the kitchen to find his sisters-in-law and brothers sitting at the table. The boys were getting ready to go out in the fields.

"Thomas, we are so sorry we did not tell you about Momma. She begged us to keep quiet and we felt we had to honor her wishes. We prayed you would be able to come home soon so you could see her." Seth said.

"See and here you are!" Andrew responded.

"But what if I had not come home....would one of you had called me to tell me about her?" His voice was wrought with emotion.

"We did what was best and you are here and that is what is important," Marie spoke with all the tenderness of the sister he loved and adored.

"You are right, I am sorry. But we have to persuade her to come to New York with me!" Thomas spoke a little too loudly as Nicole looked at him with her look. "Sorry, I did not mean to be so loud, but I just want to do something."

"Don't you think we have all been through the very emotions you are going through? We have been to several doctors with her and they all have said the same thing. There is nothing they can do."

"She can choose to live out what is left of her life in the manner in which she chooses, or go to the hospital and be poked and prodded with the same end result. Guess which she chose?" Andrew was tender but firm.

Thomas soon heard the shrill voice of his bride. "Thomas dear, I need you." Thomas got up from the table with a roll of the eyes and headed to the bedroom.

"Something is horribly wrong with those two!" Marie whispered.

"Yeah, he married the wrong gal..." Seth spoke the words that they all were thinking.

"Yes, dear," that seemed to be the only two words he could say to Elenor that kept her from exploding.

"I don't know how much longer I can stay. We must have a plan in place so that I can get home before it is dangerous to travel." Elenor looked at him as if to demand a date at that very moment.

"Elenor, there is something you need to know. I just was told that my Momma has cancer and only a little time left here on this earth," Thomas began to cry. He tried to hide it, but his heart was broken in two.

"That is just nonsense!" Elenor said. "We will simply call Daddy and have him line up the best doctor in New York City and get her the treatment that she would never get around here. We need to take her to civilization!"

Why was it that even though Elenor seemed to be wanting to help, it felt like an insult was wrapped up in a pretty bow right along with it?

"I talked to her and the family about it and she said all the doctors came to the same conclusion. They even took her to the big fancy hospital in Nashville. I think that is where civilization is here in Tennessee." His sarcasm was not lost on her.

"I was just offering to help. If she won't go to another doctor we could at least take her to our home where she could have her own personal maid and she could be cared for in her last days."

"Oh, I know, in a civilized manner?" Thomas asked. Elenor glared at him as she slammed the door.

Everyone at the table spoke to Elenor as she walked into the kitchen. It was obvious that breakfast had been over for some time, but the girls did not hesitate to offer to prepare her breakfast. They had just cleaned up, but they wanted Elenor to be happy.

Seth was not sure how long the courtesy would last, especially if they stayed for a while. And knowing Thomas, they would be staying for a while.

CHAPTER 20
1939

The days seemed to fly by for Thomas, but they were so long for Elenor that she could hardly stand it. Every single evening Elenor asked when they were going home. And every single evening Thomas told Elenor that he would not leave his Momma, knowing that she would not have much time left.

He simply could not leave, it did not matter how much she complained. His Momma had not been at the wedding, and chances were pretty positive that she would not be around for the birth of his firstborn, and that broke his heart.

Thomas fell into the routine of being back on the farm as though he had never left. Uncle Oliver visited often and sat with Fannie on the porch talking about old times.

Thomas could tell she was getting weaker each and every day. He tried to be the one taking her into the doctor each week to get her pain meds. And each time he hoped that the doctor would say the tests were wrong and that they had made a mistake, but he knew that would not happen.

"Momma, we are just praying for a miracle," Thomas told her one night at the dinner table. Everyone agreed and said they had been praying for that since they found out about her cancer.

Andrew looked rather sullen. "What is going on with you Andrew?" Seth asked as he passed the green beans over to his brother. Andrew took the beans but did not spoon out his usual huge helping.

"Nothing."

Fannie knew when her eldest son did not eat normally and answered nothing that something was really going on.

"Son, what is it?" Fannie asked.

"What is it? Are you kidding me? Momma, you are it! We pray and pray for a miracle, we pray for a healing and each and every day you get worse. Where is that miracle? Where is that healing?"

The table grew very quiet. Even Elenor stopped her jabbering about a dress she wanted to order while she could still fit into it.

"Son….all of you. Listen to me. I am good. The miracle is that I get to be home with my family and am not stuck in a hospital bed far away unable to see all my babies. And healing? I am already healed! We just want it to be on this side of heaven."

"But truth of the matter is….when I asked Jesus to come into my heart all those years ago as a young girl, I was healed of everything that ailed me then, everything that ailed me in the past and everything that would ail me in the future. Why when I get to heaven I will be whole and complete again! That is a healing and that is ok."

"I know that truly we were not created for any kind of death. Why the good Lord created us for eternal life! And I believe with all my heart that you all know that…..but that it is hard. It would be hard for me. But remember who I will be with….your daddy…and Jesus! How can that be bad in any way?"

Every eye at the table was moist with tears, even Elenor's. Momma got up out of her chair with the strength she had not had in weeks. One by one she went to each person at the table and kissed them as she prayed God's blessings on them.

Then, without another word she went out on the front porch. "Now you all finish eating and join me out here soon," she said softly as she let the screen door shut gently.

No one said a word for a few minutes. But soon everyone was eating and kidding around like they always had done. Andrew asked Thomas to pass the green beans, and this time he put his normal huge helping on his plate.

Days turned to months and Fannie actually seemed to improve a bit. She actually outlasted the doctor's prognosis and she was not in as much pain as she had been months before.

"Another miracle," she told the girls one day as they were in the kitchen making pies.

And as those months passed, so did the opportunity to go back to New York. Elenor was not happy about it at all and told Thomas often how horrible he was to make her come out here to live and have their first baby.

But she did love the way Marie, Nicole, and Fannie doted on her. Why it was almost like having her staff at home in her own house!

"Elenor, why don't you try and make some pie crust on your own?" Fannie asked as she pointed to the flour.

"Oh no, I would never be able to do that. I have never baked anything in my life. The cooks always have handled the meals, along with the desserts," Elenor replied as she nervously looked at her sisters-in-law. She saw them roll their eyes at one another. That was all it took.

"Of course Mother Fannie," Elenor said knowing that Marie and Nicole hated that name. They both called her "momma" and they felt Elenor should do the same. But Elenor always seemed to get her way.

98

"Except this time," thought Marie to herself. She knew Thomas would not be going back to New York City anytime soon.

"Girls, let's let Elenor mix the dough, it will be good for her to learn. My heavens she just might be the best pie maker in the county, and we wouldn't even know it!" Fannie grinned.

Elenor did not let her nerves show and asked Fannie question after question as she mixed the dough. She actually thought she might be enjoying it….then…the pain came and Elenor cried out.

"Daughter, what is wrong with you? Are you in labor? You still have a few weeks left, that child needs to hang on for a while yet," Fannie said.

Marie and Nicole knew how she was and they were convinced that she was just making excuses to get out of making the pie. They expected her to do what she always did when it was time for meal prep. She would excuse herself for a nap.

"She had to think about the baby." That was her standard reply as she headed for the bedroom that she and Thomas were still occupying.

But soon the girls discovered this was not another one of her excuses. Elenor's water broke as she took another deep breath and had begun to knead the dough.

"Ahhhhhhhh, where is Thomas? This is too early, the baby cannot come now. What is going on?" Elenor was beginning to panic.

"Now child, calm down. Marie will run out to the barn and get Thomas. Nicole will get the room ready. We will send for the doctor, but with your pains coming so close already, we might not be able to wait. Now hush child. It will all be just fine!" Fannie said with all the confidence she could muster.

Elenor was so worried. Why wasn't she in New York where she knew things would be fine? These women might have to deliver her baby!

For the first time ever, she prayed to a God she really knew nothing about. "If you are real, and not just some fable, you will help me," Elenor whispered.

The girls all worked as if they had done this all their lives. Seth headed into town to see if he could find the doctor, Andrew was doing all he could do to keep Thomas calm.

"It will be all right, you know that Momma knows what she is doing. She helped with all our children and Seth and Nicole's too."

"But she wasn't sick then," Thomas added.

Thomas felt like days passed rather than just hours. As much as he got fed up with Elenor's attitude, he was so happy to be a daddy. He prayed with his brothers all through the night. The baby was early. Would it be a boy or a girl?

Most importantly, would it be all right? *My Son, I love that child more than you can imagine...I am with Elenor, the baby and you.*

CHAPTER 21
1939

Thomas evidently had dozed off. How could he possibly sleep at a time like this? He thought he was hearing the cries of a baby. Yes, the cries of his precious child.

"Come here son and meet your sweet baby girl!" Thomas ran into the bedroom. His momma picked up his baby and handed her to Thomas.

"It's a girl," Elenor told Thomas in a very weak voice.

Thomas cradled her in his arms and had never felt such unconditional love as he did that very minute. He finally understood a little bit about the depth to which his heavenly Father loved him.

"Thomas, go ahead and lay the baby in Elenor's arms. She needs to try and nurse the baby, and then she needs rest.

"Your daughter appears to be in perfect condition. I believe the dates might have been off a bit. She is healthy, her lungs are clear and she is a good size." Dr. Brown said.

As if responding to his statement, Thomas' newborn daughter pierced the air with a proclamation of her need. She wanted her momma!

Elenor took a little more time recuperating than was expected by the women of Tennessee. Marie, Nicole, and Fannie did not mind one bit, nor were they surprised. The more she napped and rested, the longer the ladies got to hold and cuddle the baby.

It had been a while since a newborn had been around the house. The color returned to Fannie's cheeks and she appeared to be growing stronger as time went on. Taking care of little Adelaide was the best medicine she could have ever had anywhere!

Elenor got up and about a little more and more each day. She did not seem to mind one bit when the girls wanted Adelaide. In fact, Thomas thought she really did not spend enough time with her. Other than nursing her, he rarely saw her with the baby.

When Thomas would come in for dinner he would always find Elenor reading, Marie and Nicole fixing dinner and his momma holding Adelaide. He was thrilled to see his mother so animated, but something seemed off.

"Elenor, sweetie.....are you all right?" Thomas asked her one evening when they were in the room. Elenor had just put the baby down for the night.

"Why of course, why do you ask?" Elenor replied as she cuddled up to her husband in their bed.

"Well, dear, you never seem to have Adelaide. I always see her with one of the others when I come in." He should have known better.

Elenor exploded. "What are you talking about? Didn't you just see me nurse her and put her down for the night? You cannot possibly expect me to keep her attached to my body all day long! You infuriate me!"

"Why if we were at home, we would have a Nannie and I would most likely not even have to do that!" Elenor violently turned the other direction so that her back was to Thomas.

"Oh great," he thought. "Now she won't talk to me for a couple of days." Then the thought came to him that silence might not be bad after all.

Thomas kept working on the farm with Seth and Andrew, Elenor kept complaining, and Fannie seemed to improve a bit more. It was "routine," but Thomas loved being home.

He was absolutely giddy about little Adelaide, and she was truly smitten with her daddy. Every evening when he came in for dinner, she reached out her arms and spent the entire night with him. She always brought a smile to his face and a hug to his heart.

Elenor...was Elenor. She had seemed to be a little more emotional the last few days if that were possible. Thomas tired of her constant mood swings.

She was always comparing her life in Tennessee to her life in New York City. She also reminded him day in and day out that they were only there for a visit, and that the visit and turned into too many months!

"Thomas, I need to talk to you," Elenor said one evening as he sat on the porch with his family and the baby. Elenor had been inside, once again excusing herself because of a headache.

"Can it wait a few minutes? Adelaide will be going down for the night and then we can talk?" Thomas asked.

"No dear....now."

Marie, Nicole, and Fannie all reached for the baby and Adelaide loved it.   She reached for her Grandma first. Thomas knew she would be occupied for a while as she was passed from aunts to uncles and back to Gram.

Thomas went inside. Elenor was in "their" bedroom. The look on her face was one that Thomas knew well. Something was wrong. Again.

"Thomas.....you know that I don't want to be here. I want to go home." Elenor sat on the chair she had insisted be in the room.

"Darling, I wish you could see Tennessee as your home. Everyone loves you here. Adelaide was born here, you have fresh air and the beautiful countryside. How could New York City be any better for Adelaide?" Thomas walked closer to her chair.

"Well I would rather have our baby in New York, I would hate to have another one here on this bed again!" Elenor began to weep.

Thomas was not sure if he actually heard right. "Another baby?" Thomas thought to himself. "Sweetheart, what are you trying to say?"

"I am expecting a child you thoughtless man, we are having another baby!!" Elenor began to cry and wail. "I don't want to be pregnant again, especially here! The babies will only be a year apart. I have to get back to New York. I will not do this alone."

Thomas knew that she was referring to nannies, maids, and all the other staff. He also knew that she practically had that here since Marie, Nicole and his Momma took care of her and the baby. She always had an excuse to get out of work.

His momma said it was because she was embarrassed that she did not know how to keep a house. His sisters-in-law said it was because she was lazy. He honestly believed the latter.

"Elenor, let's think about this. Give me some time to digest this news. Having two children so close together will be a challenge, but we can do it."

"I will only carry this child if I can go back to New York!" Elenor exclaimed.

"Now what exactly does that mean?" thought Thomas as he reached down to hold his wife.

Elenor finally cried herself to sleep. Thomas was basically in shock. He walked out onto the porch where Seth had Adelaide in his arms fast asleep.

"Lord have mercy, Thomas what on earth is wrong now?" Andrew asked as he put his coffee cup down. Thomas' brothers were the only ones still up.

"We heard the wailing and gnashing of teeth," Seth quietly said.

"Well, brothers.......I cannot believe what I am about to say. But we may be heading back to New York!" He gently picked up his baby girl and walked into his room to put her in the crib like he did every night. His brothers were speechless, but not at all surprised.

CHAPTER 22
1939

The next several days were spent preparing to leave. Thomas saw that if he wanted this marriage to survive, he had no choice but to go back to New York. His heart ached.

Elenor had pointed out time and time again how much better his mother was doing and how much easier life would be.

He could pick up right where he left off at his position in the textile factory. In fact, her father was thinking about retiring and allowing Thomas to run everything.

Thomas knew that financially life would be easier, but he also knew that Elenor would always find something to complain about....that was her nature.

He also knew that she was not a follower of Christ, but simply a church attendee. She had actually told him that one evening while they laid in bed.

"Darling, I know that you love that little church we all go to, but it is so plain. It is nothing like the church we will get to go back to when we get home," she said with enthusiasm. "I don't know what it is...but I prefer the more dignified approach to religion."

"Dignified? Darling everyone is entitled to their opinion, but there is nothing wrong with plain and simple. I understand that dignified is okay too," Thomas said in a louder voice than he realized.

"Shhhh, you will wake the baby! Yes, dignified. I think God expects us to show respect and reverence. I believe he frowns upon the spontaneous 'amens' and 'hallelujahs'.

The manner in which most of the people act in a service is quite frankly appalling."

Thomas knew that she had not liked going to their church, but he had no idea she had such a strong opinion about it.

"Elenor, I am sorry that you don't care for the service and the way people act, but it is indeed a place of freedom where Jesus is present, " Thomas said with restraint.

"That is part of the problem. Everyone, including the minister, or the preacher as you call him, talk about Jesus as if he is the only way to heaven." Thomas held his breath as she continued, "You do know that he is not much more than a myth?"

Thomas really could not believe what he was hearing. She had conveniently forgotten how God had answered her prayer with the birth of Adelaide.

He thought he knew his wife, but obviously, there was plenty that he did not know anything about. *I am the way and the truth and the life.* "Lord, help me to respond in love," Thomas prayed.

"Elenor, you know that I believe that Jesus is the only way to God. He died on the cross for me...and you, our children, everyone. We can accept that and be assured of eternity in heaven." Thomas said quietly.

"Thomas you have your faith, and I have mine. There is no reason to argue about it. There are many religions and many thoughts about Jesus. I know he was a special man, but this fable about the cross? I am just not sure how I feel about that."

"So end of discussion." Elenor finished the conversation and rolled over to face the wall. "Good night my love."

Thomas laid there unable to sleep. What had just happened? How had he missed this?

"You messed up Thomas, you had to get married and you rushed through it." Thomas cringed. While he knew he had rushed through it, he also knew that guilt and condemnation were not from the Father.

"Lord, please help me. Show yourself to Elenor, let her know how much you love her. And Lord, please protect our baby girl and our unborn child." Thomas knew more than ever, he had to trust his Lord.

Thomas felt he had finally gone to sleep when the sun began to rise and the rooster began to crow, announcing the start of a fresh, new day. *My mercies are new every morning.* He was so glad of this reminder on this day. God was so faithful.

He left Elenor in bed sleeping. The rooster never seemed to bother her once she got used to him. She had added a sleep mask and simply blotted out the world.

She even blotted out Adelaide if she woke up crying. That task was left up to Thomas. It did not matter that he had to get up at dawn. She was his child too. And he loved her so much that any extra time spent with her was a sheer joy, no matter what time of the day it was.

"Good morning son!" Fannie said as Thomas entered the kitchen with Adelaide in tow.

"Elenor sleeping in again I assume?" said Marie with her usual spark of sarcasm.

"Yes, and I might as well tell all of you while you are here in the same room. Seth and Andrew already know....we are heading back to New York." The girls' expressions said it all. Fannie acted as if she already knew about this.

"Son, you have to do what is best for your family," his momma said with compassion.

"Did Seth and Andrew tell you anything?" Thomas asked.

"No, brother, we decided that this news should come directly from you," said Seth as he walked in the door.

"Is there more news than you moving back to New York?" Nicole asked.

"Yes," Thomas took a deep breath. "Elenor is expecting our second child." No one said a word, no one had to.

Finally, Fannie broke the silence. "Congratulations son! You are such a good daddy. Adelaide has been such a blessing, and this little one will be as well. Now we understand why Elenor feels she should move back." Everyone else in the room also offered their congratulations.

A couple of days passed by as they all prepared for the trio to leave. Marie and Nicole had a hard time hiding their tears. They could not bear the thought of their niece leaving and being raised in New York City.

They both held their tongue and remained very quiet. Fannie tried to be as content as possible, but she was concerned as well.

The boys had left for the fields one morning after breakfast. Adelaide was eating and laughing as she set in her high chair. Marie, Nicole, and Fannie were busy cleaning up and beginning to get ready for the day's canning.

"Help!!!!!!" the blood-curdling cry came from Elenor. "Help!!!" The girls ran into the room as Fannie pulled little Adelaide from her chair.

"Momma, I am going to head to town to get the doc, I think Elenor is about to lose the baby," Marie yelled frantically as she ran out the door.

Fannie handed Adelaide to Nicole as Thomas was walking in the door.

"What is going on? I was in the barn and thought I heard screaming!"

"Son, take your daughter, your wife may be losing the child."

The doctor arrived in record time. He just happened to be down the road at the neighbors. He was getting ready to pull out as Marie drove by.

"Doc, I think Elenor is about to lose the baby!" she yelled through her window. He did not say a word as he got in his car and took off for the farm.

The doctor spent a couple of hours with Elenor before he came out to talk to Thomas.

"Thomas, Elenor did not lose the baby." Thomas was so relieved. "But, she is on absolute bed rest the remainder of this pregnancy. She said you were about to travel back to New York City. I told her that if she made that trip she would lose this child. I think you need to go in there now."

Thomas knew that this would not be an easy conversation. Even at the risk of their child's life she obviously would want her way. He prayed he would somehow be convincing.

CHAPTER 23
1939

It was the longest six months of his life. They were all at Elenor's beck and call. They had become the house-staff she had talked about that would serve her in NYC. Thomas knew she was justified, and he wanted his baby protected, but she took too much satisfaction in it.

Everyone knew that, but for the most part, did not complain. Oh, he heard the girls talking to one another one day while they were hanging out laundry, and he had to agree with them. She was impossible.

His family did not like confrontation, but they also liked to talk things out before they became consumed with bitterness and misunderstanding.

Their typical place of discussion was the kitchen table in the mornings. This morning the topic came out of Marie's mouth with a lot of bitterness. Thomas had never heard her speak about someone in this manner. "I am sorry Thomas, but if your wife rings that cowbell one more time today....I might not be responsible for my actions."

"We don't mind helping her, we understand the situation. And you know that we love taking care of our sweet niece, but this constant ringing for no real reason has got to stop! She truly seems to enjoy having us wait on her!" Nicole could not hold back any longer.

Thomas had to agree. "I will talk to her. The good news is she is about to deliver. I know it has been an awful long six months, but just hang on a few more days. And I will speak to her about it."

Thomas did not want them to know that he had already talked to her about it several times, but it obviously did no good. That fact would not go over too well.

"We can hang on son. I have a feeling it won't be long now," Fannie said. As if she was listening to the conversation, Elenor began wailing.

"Thomas, Thomas, I think the baby is coming!" And she was right.

For such a tough pregnancy, the birth was relatively easy. A sweet little girl came into the world some four hours later. She was healthy and looked just like her big sister. Thomas could not have been any prouder.

Elenor was so excited to be able to get out of bed that the next morning she actually joined them for breakfast. Thomas had already brought Adelaide to the table, and Elenor walked in carrying the new baby. The shock on their faces must have been quite evident.

"I know that you are all surprised to see me this early. I realize that I should still be resting." The girls almost giggled. "But I thought it was time to get up and get moving around. I also think we have decided on a name….this is Audrey Sue."

Fannie was the first to say she adored the name. The others knew that Thomas wanted the baby named after their momma. But as usual, Elenor got her way.

It was amazing how quickly Elenor's strength returned. But everyone soon learned why. She was ready to head back to NYC now that the baby had been born and she was no longer required to stay in bed. In less than a week, they would all be gone.

All of the family had such mixed emotions, not wanting the girls to leave. But they had to admit they would not miss the extra work that Elenor's presence had brought.

Farm life was busy enough without having to be on Elenor's "staff."

The car was packed and ready to go. Thomas knew that his mother had been looking bad again, but he assumed it was just her hard work and age catching up with her. The family was saying their goodbyes when Sheriff Oliver drove up.

"I cannot believe you all are going back to New York, especially knowing about your Momma and all." Thomas looked at his brothers.

"What have you kept from me now?" Thomas' eyes grew in size at the thought of what was happening.

"Son, we did not want to keep it from you. But you have been delayed so many times from going back to New York and I tried to keep you here the very first time you were planning on going."

Fannie took a deep breath. "It appears as though my cancer might be back. But I will know more in a few weeks. Now you go on. I will let you know what I find out." Elenor was in the car ready to go.

"Sweetheart, we cannot go to New York. Momma is sick again and we might lose her," Thomas told Elenor as he lifted the luggage into the car.

"Dear, I am headed to NYC with or without you. My father is not well either, so it is time to go check on him. You stay here and we will take the train. In fact, I already bought tickets and the train leaves in an hour."

Thomas should not have been surprised by the revelation. Elenor had already chosen to take the girls back to New York, and she was going to have her way, again. But this time her way included his girls and he was not happy about that.

"Look, Thomas, just let me go for a few weeks. Daddy has not even met his granddaughters, and like your mother, it might make him feel better. Surely your good Christian attitude could not deny him that?" Elenor knew what she was doing.

Thomas recognized the manipulation, but he had to agree with Elenor.

"You are right, but only a few weeks, okay?"he asked as she boarded the train with his beloved girls.

"Darling, yes, of course."

Somehow he knew he would not see his children for a while, but maybe he was not giving her enough credit he thought as he walked away from the train holding back the tears.

CHAPTER 24
1940

Esther soon learned that Thomas was married, but his wife, Elenor, did not like Tennessee, its weather, and the lack of "sophistication." After their second daughter had been born, she went back east to "take care of her ill father." That had been over a year ago.

She had not returned and he rarely heard from her unless it was about the children. He offered to go get them, but she made excuses and said that her father was not ready to be alone.

Thomas missed his girls so much but honored his wife's wishes. He had one picture of them that he carried with him everywhere. He was a good father but was not given the chance to love his girls like he wanted to do.

His last letter was answered with a simple "I will let you know if you need to come here or if we will be home. I am not sure what the future holds for us."

This simply broke Thomas' heart. And although he wanted to go and get his daughters, he did not want to disrupt their settled lives. He was so torn and wanted to do what was best for them.

He told Esther that he felt like he would be served with divorce papers soon. He also knew she would never come back to Tennessee. Each passing day assured him of this fact.

She did not need him, nor his money. Her father had more money than he knew what to do with and that did ease Thomas' mind. He missed his girls and he was guilt ridden.

Thomas had worked for and lived with Mr. Gold and then met Elenor. He was confident that the children did not want for anything. Elenor told him not to send money, that all was well. He sent as much as possible anyway.

He planned several visits, but his momma passed away when one was scheduled and Elenor labeled it as abandonment. She made sure he did not see the children after that incident. His hands were indeed tied.

Thomas admitted to Esther that he did not love Elenor anymore, in fact, he was not sure if he ever loved her. He hated himself for that admission.

He had rescued and then worked for her father. He always felt that Elenor's father wanted her to marry Thomas, and Elenor's father always got his way.

But he knew he would always feel the connection to her because of the children. He felt like a failure as a father and with his upbringing knew first hand how important a father was in a child's life.

"But it is not your fault Thomas," Esther would remind him again and again. They talked for hours on end. Thomas and Esther seemed as if they had known each other a lifetime.

"What are we doing?" Thomas asked Esther one evening.

"I am not sure....I am not sure," was her reply.

Initially, Thomas had fixed the roof, then began work on all the other things that needed to be taken care of around the place. He came every afternoon after work and even spent his weekends with the family.

Joseph loved having another "man" around and told his mother often. Ruby Kay and little Annie simply adored "Mr. Thomas" and the feeling seemed mutual.

The girls must have reminded him of his own. He was wonderful with them and taught them all so much. Esther knew that the children missed their father, and even though they had Uncle Oscar, Thomas seemed to slip right into the role with ease.

One evening after Thomas had left Joseph asked the question that Esther knew was coming...

"Momma, is Mr. Thomas going to be our new Pa?" Esther's heart swelled, for she wanted to say yes so badly.

The truth was they knew until Elenor signed the papers Thomas was still married.

"I don't know what is going to take place, sweetie. Right now let's just enjoy having Mr. Thomas around, okay?"

People around town always loved Esther. Thomas had gained the respect of all those around as the new county sheriff. He was fair, worked hard and helped others. The fact that he was a nice looking single man was not lost on the other single women in town either.

Town folks did not want Esther to be alone any longer and Thomas appeared to be the answer to her prayers. He never told anyone what was really going on in his life. Everyone assumed they were a couple soon to marry.

Thomas went with Esther and the children to church every Sunday. Thomas attended every school function and even offered to help the men when they said they needed to build an addition onto the school.

They were a "family" in every sense of the word and it felt right to Esther and Thomas...except for that one little thing. He needed to be divorced and felt extremely guilty because of his wedding vows.

Months passed by and now it was Anne's turn to ask the inevitable.

"Esther" Anne said one morning over coffee. "Oscar and I simply love Thomas and the way he treats you and the children. But honestly, what is going on with you two?" Tears streamed down Esther's face.

"Oh sweet friend, I did not mean to upset you." Esther was now sobbing uncontrollably. "Esther, Esther...oh dear what can I do?" She got a cool rag and a glass of water. Eventually, Esther began to calm down.

"Oh honey, it is none of my business. I am so sorry I asked." Esther had never shared Thomas' situation with Anne or Oscar. In fact, to her knowledge, no one knew anything about Thomas and his life.

He had moved away from his hometown after his Momma passed away and he and his brothers sold the family farm. Esther said nothing, but her face spoke volumes.

"Esther, what is wrong with you? You look like you've taken ill. In fact, you haven't looked like yourself for several weeks."

Even before the reply came out of her mouth Anne knew the secret that Esther was carrying.

"Anne, I am with child." Anne began to weep right along with her best friend.

.

CHAPTER 25
1940

"Have you told Thomas?" asked Anne.

"No, I have not found the proper time to do so."

"Honey, you know that he will want to marry you right away. He won't want you to feel any shame, and he loves you and the children so much. These things happen."

"Oh Anne, I love him so much. And I know he loves me and the children. I just don't want to make him feel like he has to marry me and take on all the responsibility just because I am expecting."

"I want him to ask me because he loves me. Taking on the children is enough pressure without the thought of having yet one more mouth to feed."

Esther still did not share the fact that Thomas was actually married. What would Anne and Oscar think about her then? Their opinion about Thomas would certainly change. Anne's heart was broken for her friend...and in all honesty, herself.

"Esther, you know how special children are," her voice was even softer now. "He won't think twice."

Esther just cried harder. "If I could only share the truth," thought Esther as her tears mingled with her friend's tears. "How will I ever do that?"

That evening after dinner Anne shared with Oscar. He too was heartbroken, for Esther and for their own situation. He knew how badly Anne had wanted children for so many years. And, he had to be honest, it broke his heart as well. Anne's head was down as she sat on the chair in the front room knitting.

"I want to be happy Oscar, but my heart is so broken. My heart seems so empty. Why can't we have a baby? We have tried and tried and now I am too old. Esther has three and did not mean to get herself in this condition. It was an 'accident' she said. How can a baby ever be an 'accident'?" Anne just wept.

Oscar had no words. He had tried to comfort his wife for years, all the while hurting himself. How he wanted to be a daddy! But they were certain it was to never be. The pain was so intense that it hurt physically.

They had wrestled with the fact that maybe they were not to have children, and battled everyone's opinion on the what, why and how to.

Oscar and Anne loved Esther's children like their very own. They helped children all over the town. No one ever really knew everything they did in the entire county, much less the town.

The school teacher, Mrs. Rushing, knew she could always call on the couple if a child had any kind of need. Several times throughout the years they had even invited children into their own home to live until situations could be stable for the child.

One time a young woman from their church had died during childbirth. The father was heartbroken and disappeared. He was a fine young man but did not know what to do with his grief.

"Can you take in Mary Beth's baby girl?" the doctor asked Oscar one day in the hardware store. The doctor made it clear that the little girl had no one.

"Of course!" agreed Oscar and Anne.

They loved that baby girl and even called her "Grace." "That fits her so well," Anne said while cradling the sweet child.

They raised her as their own for six months. However, no papers had ever been signed, so when Grace's father came back with a new bride in tow....he had full rights to his daughter. He took her and left town with Grace's new mother.

Although somehow they knew it was best for Grace to be with her father, Oscar and Anne were simply heartbroken. That had been several years ago....and yet, they continued to help orphaned and abandoned babies in spite of their personal pain.

Time and time again they gave up their time, resources and love to those who needed it most. They became the stability for so many children, and their mothers as well.

"I hate to say this Oscar," Anne said one evening as they talked in their bed. "But it is not fair." She cried herself to sleep. Oscar did too, Anne just did not know it.

CHAPTER 26

1940

Anne avoided Esther for two weeks. She simply could not bring herself to check in on her friend. Seeing her would bring on that wretched pain. A pain that remained and intensified daily.

It felt as if someone was taking a sharp knife and rotating it slowly in her heart. The pain compared to when Grace left their home. Nothing would even dull it.

She simply could not stand seeing her friend, knowing she was expecting a child that she was not excited to raise. "Lord, why are you doing this to me?" she thought over and over.

She couldn't even pray anymore, or was this truly what prayer was...dialogue with a Father who understood with no words actually spoken? *I am not doing this to you daughter. This is just part of life and the choices people make. I will never, ever leave you.*

"Anne, Anne....you have to go check on Esther!" shouted Oscar as he ran from the yard to the front porch one afternoon. "Something must be terribly wrong. I have not seen Thomas in several weeks. He has not been in town and the assistant is doing the sheriff'n duties."

"I passed by the house and I heard someone sobbing through the open window. I can't tell if it is one of the children or Esther herself. But something is terrible wrong."

They ran to their best friend's home, hoping to find that little Annie had just scraped her knee while falling on the gravel, but in their hearts, they were afraid that would not be the case.

"Oh Oscar, I have been so selfish! What if Esther has needed me and I have not been there because I have been feeling sorry for myself? I will never forgive myself if something horrible has happened. I am just pitiful! Lord, Lord...please forgive me." *You have already been forgiven daughter.*

As they ran up the porch steps and as they stood at the door, they witnessed Esther's distress.

"What am I going to do Lord, what am I going to do?" She was on her knees weeping as she prayed. She looked absolutely miserable. Then she glanced up at the door.

"Oh Esther, we did not mean to interrupt you, but we heard crying and had to come to check on you and the children." Anne cried as she ran into the house to Esther's side. They both wept together as Oscar stood in the doorway, not knowing what to do with two crying women.

"Esther, I am so sorry. I have been so selfish. Let's get you up to the table so we can talk."

The ladies sat at the table as Oscar poured them all a glass of water. "Now, tell us what is wrong darlin," whispered Anne.

Esther began. "Well, I found the proper time to tell Thomas about our situation. He had not been coming like regular and seemed to always have an excuse. I was afraid he knew I was hiding something from him and wanted to start and deal with our issue as soon as possible. It turns out that I was not the only one hiding something. He had been speaking to his wife the last month.

Anne tried to keep from gasping as she placed her hand over her own mouth.

"His wife?" Oscar whispered. Esther felt so ashamed.

"I never told you because as far as Thomas was concerned he was divorced. It has been almost two years and he had gone ahead and sent divorce papers out to her."

"Out where Esther? What has been going on?" Anne asked very quietly. She felt horrible for her dear friend and never imagined the extra heartache she was going through.

Her heart had to have been plagued with so much. Esther was an honorable woman, and not only was she pregnant, but Thomas was married.

"She never signed or sent back the divorce papers. She wants him back. She wants him to come out east and live in the house her father left her and start all over! She went back there when her father took ill and right after their second child was born."

"Thomas has a wife and children?" Oscar simply could not hide his shock. "How could he do this to you Esther? Where is he? I need to give him a piece of my mind." Oscar felt his fists balling up and the anger in his heart.

"Now Oscar, calm down and let Esther finish." Anne grabbed Esther's hand and patted it gently. "Take another drink and go on sweetie." Anne knew exactly how to make people feel at ease when they were in pain.

Oscar sat in a chair at the table to listen to the rest of Esther's story. "He decided that he should do it for the sake of the children."

Esther sobbed as she finished, "What am I going to do? Everyone in town will know that I am pregnant! I can hear it now, 'that poor widow woman went and got herself pregnant, what was she thinking?"

"Esther, how long ago did Thomas leave? Have you heard from him at all?" Anne asked.

"No, I have not heard a thing in a few weeks."

"I can't believe he would leave you after you told him about the baby!" Oscar began to pace.

"Well...honestly....I did not tell him," Esther whispered.

"What?" Anne cried.

"No, I would not use the fact that I was pregnant to keep him here when he wanted to be with his own children. We were together only two times. I wanted him to go back to his wife to see how he really felt."

"Esther, you denied the man the truth. He has a child he knows nothing about and he may never come back now." Oscar murmured.

Esther sighed, "I simply could not handle the guilt anymore. We were together twice about seven months ago! We talked and knew we could not be together again until we were married...whenever that would be. So if he thinks poorly of me I deserve it." Esther started crying again.

At this point, Oscar had nothing more to say. He was simply in shock. But Anne did what Anne always did...she comforted Esther. Anne was such an encourager, it came naturally. It wasn't in what she said, it was the unconditional love that she shared with those around her that were hurting.

There really wasn't anything to say, Esther was feeling horrible and nothing would erase that pain. They sat there for a while and little Annie walked in the door.

"Momma, whas wong?" she asked innocently. Anne lifted her up in her lap and gave her a hug.

"Nothing that a little love cannot fix sweetie." Little Annie jumped down, gave her momma a hug and ran back out to play.

"Oh Anne, if it could only be that easy." Esther shuttered, she felt like she had no more tears. What was going to happen now?

CHAPTER 27
1941

The days seemed to fly by as Esther grew with the child. She was able to hide it quite well with her large smocks and aprons, and Oscar or Anne ran her town errands and delivered her pies.

The children never seemed to notice, except for Joseph, who often made the passing comment that "Momma seems to be eating too many of her own pies." He would laugh as Esther hoped he would not notice the truth.

As the time drew near, Esther and the children asked the Bells over for dinner. "It is a 'celebrtchen' dinner" little Annie yelled as she jumped up and down. Anne and Oscar didn't quite know what to make of this celebration.

"What are we celebrating Annie?" Annie shrugged her shoulders and ran off with "Wufas."

"Well, she is not a lot of help," Oscar said with a grin.

"You will find out soon enough." Esther turned back to her cooking.

Dinner was grand. Ruby Kay helped make the biscuits, Joseph sat the table as Esther fried the chicken. Annie entertained everyone with her stories, even though they could not understand most of her words.

She still had quite a way with stories. And to think at one time everyone was afraid she might never talk, at this rate that was not going to be an issue! Anne had to chuckle at the thought as Annie added one more puppy to her story. Anne simply adored her little namesake.

Rufus was even allowed to stay in the house.

"Well, something special is going on if Rufus has been allowed to stay in the kitchen!" Oscar scratched Rufus' ears.

"He gets to sleep with us too Uncle Oscar!" Ruby Kay offered.

"Well as long as he doesn't make a mess he can," Esther told the children.

"Celebrtchen!" little Annie sang. Ah, to have the joy of a child around again thought Anne.

"These here pies are the best you have ever baked I do believe," commented Oscar as he took another big bite of cherry pie. "This must be some celebration! I love the cherry pie, but you baked my favorite pecan...and I have not even taken a slice of it yet. Boy oh Boy, it feels like Christmas!"

Joseph laughed. "Uncle Oscar, you eat more pies and you will get as big as Momma." Joseph grinned, he knew something was not right, but he did not know exactly what it was.

"Now Esther, what exactly are we celebrating?" Oscar interrupted.

"Children, run upstairs and get ready for bed. Uncle Oscar will come up and tuck you in soon." Kisses were shared with Momma and Aunt Anne and off they went.

Uncle Oscar always told funny bedtime stories, and Esther hoped he could sidetrack Joseph with talk about upcoming hunting or fishing.

She knew that Oscar would be there a while, especially with Annie adding her gibberish to the stories. Someday she might just write a book if her imagination kept growing!

"Anne, do you want another piece of pie?" asked Esther.

"No, I want you to tell me what this is all about!" she replied. "Is Thomas coming back?" Anne asked with hopeful anticipation of a positive answer.

"I have not heard from him Anne and I am not getting my hopes up. I have to go on with our lives and have had to do a lot of thinking and praying. You know that I have been praying about my situation constantly."

"I think I truly know what it means now when the Bible says to 'Pray without ceasing' I am horribly ashamed of the condition I got myself in, much less with a married man."

Esther paused to take a breath. "But the good Lord has forgiven me and shown me that giving this little one life is the most important thing ever. But I simply don't have the means in which I can raise another child alone."

"Esther, oh sweet friend, I have been praying for you constantly too. I am so glad that you recognize the Lord's forgiveness. He does forgive you."

Thinking about her own life, she continued. "We all do things we are not proud of in our lives, but we know that forgiveness is ours if we have accepted the Lord Jesus into our hearts. I think the biggest problem we often have is forgiving ourselves." Esther nodded her head in agreement.

"You know that I love you two and that you are the best friend a person could ever have…why without you and Oscar I don't know how we would have made it after William died." Esther whispered.

"I was lying in bed last night thinking about all the sweet memories we have before he died. Anne, you were here when all of the children were born, when we celebrated birthdays and Christmases together.

You aren't just my best friends….no, you are truly family." Tears began to slip down her face as she grabbed one of Anne's hands across the table.

Anne took Esther's other hand in hers. "Anne, you know how you think that my children are a gift to you?"

129

"Yes," Anne replied shakily, not wanting to possibly consider what was going through her mind.

"Well, I have a special gift I want you to have... forever." Esther's tears increased.

"What? you don't mean...." Anne uttered.

"Yes, my friend...I do. I want you to take this gift I give. And give this child all the love and care you have to give."

"Esther, think about what you are saying!" Anne said, all the while hoping she wasn't dreaming about all this and she would wake up in her bed.

"Anne I have thought about it night after night since Thomas left. I have prayed and prayed. I simply cannot do this alone."

"I won't do it to the baby and I won't do it to the other children. It is one of the hardest decisions I have ever had to make. But, the most unselfish thing I can do for all of us is allow you and Oscar to adopt and raise this child. You two are more than ready to be a Mommy and Daddy."

"But Esther, what if Thomas comes back? What if he finds out the truth and that we have adopted his child? " Anne stuttered.

Esther answered, "I have written him a letter explaining all of it. I told him that I should have shared that I was expecting, but I knew he had to get home to his girls. I told him my plans for the baby."

"He fell in love with you two as well so he won't object. And I know with all my heart if he truly was going to come back I would have heard from him by now. I will send it to the post office as soon as you two agree to this."

Oscar hopped down the stairs only to find the two women crying in each others' arms.....again! "Lord sakes women, is that all you two do?" Both turned their head towards Oscar.

"Oscar come here and sit down," said Anne.

"Uh-oh," he thought. "I am not sure I like the sound of that," he said.

"Sweetheart, Esther has something to tell you...or to ask you really," Anne said.

"Confound it, women, would someone tell me what is going on? Is this part of the celebration you have talking about Esther?" Oscar asked.

Esther began, "Oscar, I have something precious I would like to give you if you are willing to receive it..." Oscar looked at Anne, then at Esther and back at Anne. With a nod of Anne's head as to affirm what Oscar was imagining, his face was soon splotchy with all his crying.

Of course, he had all the same questions as Anne had shared. And Esther repeated all she had told Anne. Esther had even spoken to a judge in confidence a few days ago when he was in town and had proper adoption papers drawn up.

"I want to do it the right way. The baby will officially be yours with no questions asked." Esther said.

"Momma!" yelled little Annie from upstairs. "Celebrtchen?" All three of them laughed.

CHAPTER 28
1941

Oscar and Anne could not sleep that night.

"I cannot believe this Oscar!" We are in our 50's, are we too old to raise a child?" Oscar took a deep breath.

"Sweetheart, it does sound like we are old when you say it out loud. But I don't feel old."

"How long have we waited for a child to call our own? I had given up honey, I had simply lost faith. But then I had to believe that the good Lord still loved us even if we did not have a child of our own," Anne got closer to her husband.

"Oh sweet Anne, the Lord gave us several children to love on through the years. We were faithful to love them even knowing that we would most likely not be able to keep them in our home forever. We have to trust God with this too."

They wrapped their arms around one another and dreamt about boy and girl names.

Anne was sitting at the table, Bible open and tears streaming down her face. She was trying to finish breakfast. Oscar came in from the field after early morning chores.

"Anne, I swear, those tears are going to have to dry up sooner or later. Lands sake, there has been more crying these last couple of months than there has been in our entire lifetime," Oscar said as he poured himself a cup of coffee and sat down at the table.

"Oscar, I woke up this morning so scared that I had dreamt all this. Then I realized I had not. I looked at the paper Esther gave us to sign and I realized it wasn't a dream at all."

"Ah darlin, I know exactly how you feel. As I was out this morning and saw the sun rising up high in the sky I was just pinching myself. I could not thank the Lord enough for what He had done."

"The good Lord indeed takes terrible situations and even the mistakes we have made and uses them for our good....if we let Him do it."

Anne agreed. "I know, I was just re-reading about Abraham and Sarah. God had it taken care of and they kind of meddled in it didn't they?"

"Yes, ma'am, but God had it all taken care of...just like he does now. We are getting ourselves a baby!"

Oscar took Anne's hands in his own and pulled her to her feet. "I love you, Mrs. Bell."

"I love you too Mr. Bell." *I love you both with such unconditional love.*

The task at hand soon became how they were going to explain about the baby. They wanted to protect Esther and the children, and yet they did not feel right lying.

"It ain't no body's business," Oscar exclaimed one evening as they finished supper with Esther and the children.

"Joseph, have you worked on those spelling words?" asked Esther.

"No ma'am," he said. "Then head up to the bedroom and take the girls with you."

"I'll be the teacher," said Ruby Kay with authority. Joseph just rolled his eyes and laughed.

Esther, Anne, and Oscar continued their conversation out of the earshot of the children.

"Honey, but people are going to ask how we got a baby, and really I might ask the same thing. They aren't trying to be ugly, they are just curious," said Anne.

Esther cleared her throat.

"Why not tell the truth, just not the details? A great friend was in a horrible situation with no husband and asked you to adopt the baby."

"That is the truth, and I have not been in town for a while anyway so no one will notice," said Esther.

"What about the children though?" Anne was so concerned about them.

"Hmmm, I have been thinking about that too. Maybe I could stay at your house. We can tell the children that you are taking care of me because I am not feeling well. And that my dear friends is the truth," Esther said as she put her hand on the small of her back.

"Oscar, you could stay with the children and Joseph can keep going on to school and the girls can go and play at Molly's. They do that once a week and that will seem normal to them."

Oscar thought for a minute. "I think that will work gals."

Esther grinned, "Well for goodness sake, I cannot have a baby without my Anne there right by my side anyway. And Dr. Turner said he would come out and deliver the baby as well."

"Then it is settled," Oscar said. "Now little one, let's get this show on the road soon."

CHAPTER 29

1941

Planning on the birth of a baby is never easy, but especially when you are trying to keep it from the children that are around every day. Joseph seemed to know something was not right, so he seemed to help with the girls.

Esther knew when she thought the baby would come but had not seen the doctor on a regular basis. She ate right and thankfully had no problems, but there was still fear in her heart at the thought. What if she had hurt the baby in some way by not seeing the doctor more often she thought.

"Nonsense Esther," Anne said. "You have done all the right things, nothing different. And you did see Dr. Turner a couple of times. He would have told you if he thought there was a problem of any kind."

"When you are close to the time of the baby hopefully the children will be in school and you can just come to our house."

"Remember, Oscar is staying with the children and telling them that I am taking care of you because you have fallen ill." Joseph seems to helping with the girls, he seems to have such an old soul," Anne stated.

"Just like William," Esther replied.

Esther always wore smocks and an apron, so she really did not look like she was expecting. Early one morning while she was fixing breakfast for the children the pains began.

"Momma, are you all right? Your face looks really funny," said Joseph.

"Oh sweetie, I am just tired….I might be coming down with something. You finish your breakfast and you head on out to school." Esther sat down.

Joseph looked at her with grave concern.

"Joesph, first go to the phone and ask Uncle Oscar and Aunt Anne to come over."

"Momma, you look really sick," he said. He quickly ran to the phone. Joseph then headed on out the door to fetch Oscar as he walked up.

"Children, your momma will be fine. Now Joseph go on to school and girls, let's go on to Molly's."

"I may not be here when you get home, so mind Uncle Oscar in case I'm gone." Esther tried to stand straight in the midst of another pain.

"Gone????" little Annie whimpered.

"Are you gonna go to heaven like Pa ?" asked Ruby Kay in her small voice.

"Oh no honey, your momma is just ailing a bit, she will be fine Aunt Anne is on her way too." Oscar did his best to comfort the girls.

Joseph reached for Annie and Ruby Kay's hands and reassured them as only a big brother could do. "Momma will be fine with Aunt Anne."

"Anne, I do believe this child has decided to make its appearance today!" Esther whispered through another labor pain.

"I sent Oscar into town to fetch the doctor," Esther said. "I did not want to call and have that operator hear about it. Why goodness, she would spread it all over town!" "Oh, dear one, I am glad you did see the doctor, he is bound to be quiet about all this. I am sure he will be here soon." Anne prayed that what she said was indeed the truth.

They drove the Dodge to the Bell's house, it was not that far, but Anne feared that Esther might not be able to walk even the small distance. They walked onto the porch as another pain came.

As they walked up the stairs Esther had to stop and catch her breath.

"You can do this Esther, you know that the spare bedroom is not that far," Anne said gently.

Esther settled into the soft bed as the pains increased in strength and came more often.

"Anne, it is not going to be long now. You know I had all my babies quick and it seems this one isn't going to be much different."

Anne had helped when the other children were born, but she had never been alone. Dr. Turner had always been there.

"Esther, we will take care of it whether the doctor is here or not," she said with the confidence that she actually did not possess. "Lord, help us out here....I am a little fearful," Anne prayed. *I am with you always.*

"Lord, now don't you go and complete that...until the end of days....I don't want this labor to go on that long!"

Doctor Turner walked in the door as Esther let out a loud cry.

"Sounds like we got here just in time!" Oscar said. "Straight that'a way doc."

Oscar had never heard such wailing. He sat down in the kitchen, put on a pot of coffee and waited. Seems like there was a lot of coffee drinking going on lately, and tonight was no exception.

He did not have to wait very long. Soon he heard the beautiful cries of a baby. THEIR baby. He began to tear up as Anne walked into the kitchen.

137

"She is here Oscar, our daughter has been born! A precious little girl." They fell into each other's arms imagining what it would now be like to really be parents.

"Every child is a miracle Lord, but I thank you especially for this one," prayed Anne as she and Oscar held hands and stood near the sink.

"Anne, do you think I can see her before I go back to Esther's house?"

"Let me go check honey. I want to make sure it is okay with Esther and the doctor." Soon she was back. "Come on back and meet your daughter."

Anne fell in love with the baby immediately. Esther did as well, and although she knew it was the right decision to make, it hurt her heart so much as they signed all the necessary papers.

It was almost official. Oscar would deliver the papers to the judge soon and the little girl would be their daughter.

Esther trusted God to get her through this…as did Anne.

"At least I will still be in her life Anne….at least I will get to see her grow up," Esther said through heavy tears.

"We wouldn't have it any other way" Anne replied. "Hello little one, do you know just how loved you are?"

The months turned into years, and a little girl grew by leaps and bounds. She was such a happy child. She loved her mommy and daddy, and they loved her with all their heart.

She was cherished by all those around her. While she loved school, baking with her aunt was her favorite thing to do. Her aunt was alone, her children were teenagers and not interested in baking. She loved to teach the little girl everything she knew about baking. The little girl learned so much and every day after school she cried out to her momma.

"Mommy, I don't have much homework, can I go bake now?"

"No young lady, you know you have to finish that homework first!" Her mother smiled when she thought about how happy her little girl was and how she loved her life.

CHAPTER 30
1952

One day Esther shared with Oscar and Anne that she was going to have to sell the farm and move to town. She did not want to, but the children were busy with their own lives and the cost of raising them and keeping up with the farm was just too much. She would sell the livestock and have enough to get a small place for her and the children.

"I will have too much space at the farm once the children are gone. I just don't want to depend on anyone else to keep up the farm anymore. I just can't and feel it is time to sell. "

Anne agreed. "Well, you are not going to believe this... but we have talked about the very same thing. It seems like Mr. Walker is interested in the farm, and he might be interested in yours too."

"I want to be closer to the millinery shop now and Oscar would not have to work so hard on the farm. Since he got the engineer's job for the railroad he is exhausted most of the time and I worry about his health Esther."

Mr. Walker did want both farms. He was a young man and had worked hard to earn money to purchase farmland. Anne, Oscar, and their daughter found a beautiful home on the south side of town. It was near the train station and the millinery shop.

Esther and the children found a smaller home on the South side as well. It was within walking distance for all of them. Joseph, Ruby Kay, and Annie were closer to their school and activities and Oscar and Anne's daughter could continue working in Aunt Esther's kitchen. Anne had just bought the millinery shop, and Esther was able to help out there as well.

The households were very busy over the next several days. Moving to town was a chore and with moving day around the corner, everyone seemed to be busy all day long. There was very little time for sitting, relaxing and reading.

Esther had let the mail pile up a bit, which was extremely unusual and she simply had to take time to go through it. She sat in her wingback chair next to the window and began the task at hand.

One piece of mail was a lovely card from a lady at the church who thanked her for the pie her husband had Esther bake.

"What a wonderful surprise! The best pie ever!" The next letter was from a friend that had attended church with her years ago. She was moving back to the area and wondered how things were in town?

The next letter had handwriting that did not look familiar at all. The return address was from New York. Who on earth would she be getting a letter from in New York?

For some reason, her heart began to beat a little faster than usual and she was a bit surprised. In fact, her hand began to shake. "What is this all about?" she thought as she tore open the envelope.

She began reading and her pulse quickened even more. It was a letter from Thomas' wife, Elenor! Why would she be writing Esther? Had he told her about their affair? Was Elenor trying to cause trouble?

Esther had never heard from Thomas after he left, in spite of the letter she had written to him about the baby. She did not want him to return, she just felt that he had a right to know about the baby since he was the father. He had such love for his daughters after all.

"Dear Esther,

You don't know me at all. But I truly feel I do know you. You are the woman that I should have been. I was a spoiled, rotten brat who became a spoiled, rotten adult. And poor Thomas had to put up with it the majority of his life.

You made him happy. That fact used to bring me pain to say that, but as I look back it really wasn't pain, it was jealousy. I knew Thomas never truly loved me, but once I trapped him into marriage with my Daddy's help, I knew that he was a man of integrity and he would never leave me. I was right. I left him, but he never left me.

So why am I writing you this letter? I am writing it to ask for forgiveness. Yes, forgiveness! When Thomas came back his heart was broken. You were his only true love, and I took that away from him.

I literally used our very own daughters to keep him here in New York. The only time I saw him happy is when he was with them. He tolerated me for their sake, and because he would not break his wedding vows. That was the type of man he was. Please don't ever doubt that.

The letter that you wrote to Thomas was delivered to our home. But I was always given the mail first and I hid it from him. I don't know why I did not simply burn it, but maybe there was something good inside of me just waiting to get out.

Thank the Lord He did not quit loving and pursuing me. My daughters persuaded me to attend a Billy Graham Crusade with them in the city one evening while vacationing.

They are very much like Thomas, and love on people… actually love on the unlovable. I never understood how or even why they bother to do that, but I digress.

In 1949 Adelaide, Aubrey and I took a trip to Los Angeles. After two days of begging me, I decided to attend the crusade with them. My life has never been the same. I walked the aisle that night and made Jesus my Savior, Lord, and King. It was like nothing I had ever experienced. I had undeniable peace.

We came home and I knew that I had many "fences to mend." I had been so unkind to so many people over the years. I literally wrote out a list of all those I could remember that I had wronged. Your name was on the list. But I kept pushing it to the bottom.

As you can well imagine, it took a while to get to everyone. In fact, I am still working on it and working on myself as well. The girls were talking with me one evening during dinner. They knew the story and asked if I had written to you yet. I had to answer truthfully that I had not written.

I could not forgive him or you either. I had left and told him that I would not come back and that I wanted a divorce. I realized that I had set him free. I had hate and unforgiveness towards you. That was not hurting you, only eating me alive as a cancer can do.

Although I feel like what happened between the two of you was wrong, I understand how it happened. I just wish I could have given that apology to Thomas. I made him live with guilt the rest of his life.

After Thomas confessed the affair to me and asked my forgiveness, I denied him that. In fact, I held it over his head his entire life. That is something I will always have to live with.

I know that if you expose the darkness to the light it will have no power over you. So, I forgave each of you. Then I penned this letter. The girls knew this would be very freeing to me, and it is now. But I know how it will rear its ugly head over and over to remind me how terrible I was to him and his child.

Thomas was killed in the war and never got to read your letter. For that, I will be eternally sorry. He never knew about his child. I kept that from him.

He would have supported the child I have no doubt. But I could not bear sharing him with anyone, and I did not want him coming back to Tennessee, even to see the child.

I have enclosed a sizable cashier's check for Thomas' child. I am not sure if it was a girl or boy, but the girls and I were in agreement that the child deserved part of their father's inheritance.

He worked so hard. He also received money from my daddy. My daddy adored Thomas and I believe he truly strived to be the man that Thomas was to him.

So please accept this gift, and allow us the blessing of giving it. I know that the good Lord has plans for it far beyond anything we can see. And who knows, maybe someday we can meet, or at least the girls might meet their half-sibling. They would love that I know.

Again, Esther, I am so, so sorry. Maybe one day we will meet on this side of heaven as well.

Humbly,
Elenor"

Esther closed her eyes. She should not be in awe of what the Father had done. He was indeed love.

CHAPTER 31
1981

I heard the knock at the door as I began to tear open the envelope. I laid the partially opened envelope on the table. "Now who could that be?" I thought to myself.

I was so looking forward to my time alone today. Although if I am really being honest with myself, my actual alone time is pretty darn lonely.

I missed Mark, no matter how hurt or mad I was. I missed the easy way we could discuss anything years ago. I missed his constant aggravation and that little-crooked smile he showed when he was being mischievous. But I had to put all that behind me now and get on with my new "normal", my new life.

"Ok, Ok....I am coming!" I shouted as the knocking got louder. "My goodness, give me a minute." I opened the door.

"Mark! What are you doing here?" I said as I looked at his face. He had been crying and something was terribly wrong. "What is wrong? Come in, come in," I said with such comfort that it surprised me.

I will never forget that look on Mark's face as long as I live. As a little girl, I remember the pain that I could not understand when my Daddy passed away; and most recently, Mom's death. Although I knew she was not in good health and I expected her death, I am not sure one is ever really ready.

"Mattie, I am sorry I came here....I just could not think of anywhere else to go," his shoulders began to shake. I led Mark to the living room couch and offered him a cold drink.

"Do you want a glass of water or some iced tea?" Buster was so glad to see him. He was all over his lap, licking his face. He too knew something was horribly wrong. Dogs always seem to know when things are wrong. And Buster seemed even more intuitive.

Mark got quiet and just sat for a minute. I really felt I should give him some time to compose himself before I started asking questions.

"How could I be sitting here wanting to comfort this man?" I thought. *Listen to him. Let me love him through you.*

"Dad.....I can't believe it, Mattie. Dad had a sudden heart attack. He tried to talk to me the last couple of times we saw each other. He was so upset with me for what I did to you and the kids."

Mark was beyond heartbroken. "I was feeling sorry for myself and did not pay any attention to how he looked. He had been really tired for several months, but I just thought it was his age and all the work he has been doing since Mom had been sick."

"Mark, where is he? Where is your mom?" Mattie whispered. The tears immediately reappeared. Mark was trying to be strong, but he was a broken man. He had been broken the last several months, but this was even more so.

"Mom is with Linda. Mattie....he is gone."

"Gone?" I said with unbelief. I simply could not contain myself. Soon the tears were dripping off my chin as well. I could not believe it. Mark's dad had treated me just like a daughter. He checked on me after the divorce and always kept up with the kids.

I had not talked to Mark's mom or dad in a couple of weeks and had never made time to return their calls. That was on my list of things to do while the kids were at camp. How could this be?

Soon we were holding on to each other for dear life. All the memories we shared came crashing in on us. Our grief brought us together again. Another season of life was upon us, and we were having to deal with it like this.

After a few minutes, I pulled away.

"Mark, we probably need to get back to your mom and sister. The kids are still at camp," Mattie said. "Let's not get a hold of them yet. I want us to be able to see them face to face."

"I agree, this is not the kind of news we should give them over the phone. They have been through so much lately." Mark's words held in the air.

Then it occurred to Mark.

"Are you saying you will come with me?" he asked.

"Yes, I love your Mom and Sister....and I loved your Dad with all my heart. Since my dad had died, your Dad was the closest thing I had to a father in my adult life." I then went to find my jacket.

CHAPTER 32
1981

I got in Mark's car. "Wow, how can this be happening?" I thought to myself. "Mark, why don't you let me drive?" I glanced at his ashen face.

"Well, it actually might be a good idea Mattie"

Mark got out of the driver's seat and walked around to my side. He was truly a distraught man, and I was not sure it was just because of his father's death. I knew that we were family again for at least the next several days. But why did that bring me comfort? *My design.*

Our ride was silent. The radio was tuned to a Christian radio station, which had never been Mark's normal choice.

"Great," I thought to myself. "The Imperials singing PRAISE THE LORD….that is the last song I want to hear right now," I muttered under my breath.

I began to adjust the dial. The next pre-set station? Another one, just like the other and another Imperials song? What was going on with this man? I'M FORGIVEN. "Really, I have to hear this right now?" I thought to myself.

"Ok Lord, you have my attention." I really thought I heard *It's about time Mattie.* "Oh no, not Amy Grant!" I thought as I made a right turn into his parents' neighborhood.

I pulled the car into his parent's driveway and began to cry.

"Mattie, you don't have to go in," Mark said as he wiped the tears from my face.

"It is not your responsibility anymore."

"Nonsense." I opened the door. "I told you that I love your parents and sister and always will, that will never change."

Linda saw me and started crying again as she walked over. "Oh Mattie, thanks so much for coming over. Mom is in the kitchen and will be so glad to see you. How are you? I have missed seeing you so much."

Linda hugged me as if her life depended on it. We had been sisters for a long time and friends before that...it had been awkward with her since the divorce.

She loved her brother so much and looked up to him. She admitted she was disappointed in him but had told me several times that I should forgive him.

"God can work this out if you let Him, Mattie," she said to me time and time again.

"Not this time," was my usual reply.

"Mattie, God can heal anything," she always said. After the last conversation I had decided that nothing would ever be the same with her, she just did not understand the betrayal I felt.

I walked into the kitchen to see Betty. Ah, Betty had been the best mother-in-law anyone could ever have....when my friends complained about their mothers-in-law, I bragged on mine.

Pretty soon I learned to just keep my mouth closed. They all got really tired of hearing how fabulous she was. But she truly was just that and more.

She was a woman of God and always ready to listen and never judged anyone. She only offered advice when asked and she and I shared the "gift of sarcasm" as I often called it.

She never interfered with our relationship....ever. She never held up for her son during the whole ordeal. In fact, it was just the opposite.

She told me how sorry she was that Mark had hurt me so badly. She never offered excuses for him, and never blamed me, but she was never ugly about him either. However, she did want me to forgive him, actually the only piece of advice she offered without me asking.

"Betty, I just can't. He betrayed me and I have biblical grounds for divorce." I told her one afternoon when she came to the bakery.

"Ah, sweet girl...my prayer will never change for you two. You were meant to be together and I know God can heal even the most broken of things." Betty would always say it with a sweet smile. How could I ever get frustrated with such a loving woman?

And there she sat at the kitchen table. She had stopped crying for the moment, but the open Bible that laid on the table was evidence that the tears had been flowing heavily.

"Oh sweet Mattie," she whispered as she stood and I went into her loving arms.

"Betty, I am so sorry." I cried openly and Betty began consoling me.

"Dear one, you know I once heard that we were not created for death...that God created us for eternity. I believe this Mattie." Betty took a deep breath. "That must be why it hurts so much. I know he is with Jesus, I just wanted to be with him when we saw our Savior for the first time...."

Betty sat back down in the chair and grabbed another tissue. "Mattie, I am so glad to see you...please sit down with me." Linda offered me a cup of tea and sat at the table with us. Mark leaned against the counter.

"How are you feeling Betty....I mean physically?"

"Oh, I am fine. You know that I really thought I would be the first to go. Even though we were constantly telling each other that we would go together. Deep down we knew it would not be that way."

"But after my cancer, I just felt it would be me. Dad was exhausted, he took such good care of me through the treatments," a quiver was evident in her voice.

"Well, I am here for you guys....all of you," I said as I glanced over near the counter. "All of you." Mark's eyes met mine. Linda preceded to talk about the kids and telling them. She encouraged Betty to go up and get ready for bed.

"Oh Linda, honey...how can I ever sleep in that bed again? Through all my treatments, your daddy never left my side. He was always there trying to sleep, no matter how hard it was on him. I know he is absent from the body and all that gives me hope is knowing He is present with the Father. But boy does it hurt."

"You know what Betty?" I said without much thought.... "why don't you sleep in the guest room tonight? The kids would love to have you in their room while they were not there. I know that they would think that would make you happy."

"Yeah Mom, that is a good idea," Mark said. "Linda has to get home to the kids and I will stay down here and sleep on the couch so you won't be alone."

"My sweet children, that is such a good idea...but I have to start sometime. I will just make myself go into our bedroom and sleep in our own bed."

"Your Dad would have wanted me to be strong. And God will be laying right next to me," Betty whispered. "Just don't be surprised if you hear me crying."

Just like so many times before, Mark and I went to her and helped her up.

"We will walk you to your bedroom Mom," Mark said. Soon each of us went on one side of the lady we loved dearly and walked her back to the bedroom that would no longer be occupied by two people.

.

CHAPTER 33
1981

I was waiting in the parking lot at church for the kids to get home from camp. By now everyone in camp knew about it and my fear was that somehow the kids had found out.

But they knew from the look on my face that something was terribly wrong. I had never been very good at hiding my feelings. And yes, I am a bit sensitive. "The very thing you are gifted in my dear is the very thing that can destroy you," Betty had told me one day. Funny how one remembers things.

"Mom, what is wrong? Mom...tell us," Mary Beth said.

"I don't feel good about this," added Matthew.

"Mom, you look really sad."

We headed for the car and the kids put their bags in the trunk.

"Guys, just get in the car," I quietly said to all of them. I had wanted to wait until we made it home, but with all the news they had received lately from the divorce to my mom's death...I knew I should not wait.

"Kids, Granddad had a heart attack," I whispered.

"Ok, so which hospital is he in?" asked Michelle.

She was the youngest and I often found her with her granddad in his shed fixing fishing lures. She was still young enough to do things like that with her grandfather and not be embarrassed by it. Once the fishing lures were fixed, they were off to their favorite pond.

"Oh honey, he is in heaven...you know Granddad, he is probably fishing with a couple of the disciples about now." I tried to sound encouraging, but my words seemed hollow as I heard them all quietly weep.

"My gosh Lord, how much more do these babies have to endure?" I halfway prayed. *No height, no depth can separate them from my love.*

Matthew was trying not to cry, but it was so hard. He took a breath long enough to ask about his dad.

"Mom, how is Dad?"

"We need to be with him right now!" Mary Beth chimed in.

"Guys, dad is at work at the welding shop."

"Does that really matter? You know he wants to see us, and we have to see him, Mom. He needs us," Mary Beth pleaded. "Don't deny us that Mom".

"Wow," I thought to myself. "What had I been "denying" them since the divorce?" What a strange choice of words, or was it?

I had allowed them to see their dad whenever they wanted. I never told them about any of the things that went on between him and the other woman (I still could not say her name out loud.)

Granted I had not let the kids hang out with her kids anymore, but that was to be expected. Wasn't it? Although I had offered them several excuses as to why evidently my children never believed any of them. What did they know?

"Of course, your Dad would want to see you. We will go there before we go home." Before I could even get to a complete stop at the shop, the kids were opening the door. I wanted them to have their personal time with their dad.

They loved their granddad so much, he had been such a wonderful grandfather to them, and father to me.

"Gosh I am going to miss that man," I thought to myself as I stood looking in the window watching my ex-husband hugging and crying with his kids.

The next several days were a blur honestly. But it seemed we were a family again.

The visitation was held on Tuesday night and we all stood with Betty, Linda, her husband Peter and the entire family. And yes, even Mark. I was on one side of him and the kids would come up and stand with us off and on.

It was a very long night, but Betty was so sweet and encouraging to everyone. Never mind that she had just completed cancer treatments. She always put others before herself.

She never complained and loved everyone. Even as she sat in the chair by the casket of the love of her life. I thought how much I wanted to have that in my life. Would it ever be now?

The kids picked out some red roses. They knew roses were Granddad's favorite flowers.

"Yeah Mom, we picked out five roses," said Michelle.

"Why five?" I asked, not thinking about where they were going with this.

"Mom.....that is a silly question," she said with her typical exasperation. "We have five in our family, and each is one of us. They will be right by Grandad so he won't feel alone."

"Oh, okay," those were the only two words I could muster.

We heard story after story about John. Each one was a reminder of the true Godly man we knew. He always was surrendered to Jesus in his life, and when he wasn't he knew it.

He was never afraid to admit he was wrong. He also was not afraid to confront someone he loved when he knew they were wrong.

155

Many stories we heard came from people that we did not even know. One young man with special needs extended his hand to Betty.

"Mr. John was my friend," he stuttered. "Mr. John brought me a sandwich, an apple and even a donut every single day."

Betty asked his name. "I am Sam and Mr. John told me all the time that Jesus loved me so much."

Betty wondered, "Sam, where were you when Mr. John brought you the sandwich?"

"And the apple and the donut?" Sam added with eagerness.

"Yes, Sam, and the apple and donut," Betty responded with a smile.

"I was at my work. Mr. John would say hello to all my bosses and talk for a few minutes while I ate. Mr. John told me that he might not be there someday and it made me really sad. Then he said that God loved me and would always take care of me."

Betty wiped tears from her eyes. "Sam, how did you get here?"

"One of my bosses brought me because she knew that Mr. John would want to see me one last time." Then Sam continued down the line.

CHAPTER 34

1981

"I know you!" Sam shouted as he reached out to hug Mark.

Mark hugged Sam back and said, "I am sorry Sam, but have we met?"

Sam laughed. "Oh, no silly guy. But I know you because you look and sound just like Mr. John! Do you know that Jesus loves you?"

Mark then wiped his eyes. "Sam, I will talk to your boss and find out where I can bring your sandwich each day."

Sam smiled, "and an apple and a donut?"

"Of course," said Mark.

Mark hugged Sam and as he was on his way he sang these familiar words. "Jesus loves me this I know, for the Bible tells me so...."

Sam walked out of the funeral home with a smile on his face and a skip in his step. Everyone sitting was smiling and wiping tears at the same time. Sam seemed to understand all of this better than anyone.

The line slowed a bit at the end of visitation and Mark and I sat down in the front row. Mattie was the first to speak.

"Looks like you are going to be making a sack lunch for someone every day now."

"I am kind of used to it since I did it for years." Again more tears began to stream down Mark's face as he looked at Mattie and then the casket.

"Oh, Mattie, how I wish I could have been half the man that my dad was...." I could tell that he felt awful. He did not just feel awful about the death of his dad, but the last conversation they had with one another had not been entirely pleasant.

"I was so defensive Mattie, I would not admit to him how wrong I was about so much." His voice trailed off as words almost escaped me.

"He loved you, Mark," surprising myself with the words of comfort I had for my ex-husband.

The funeral the next day was more of a celebration than a funeral. John had always been very specific about the type of service he wanted when he died. In fact, it was all written down in his Bible and Betty knew right where to find it.

He had not missed a beat. The music was his favorite and very uplifting. He had even written a letter to be read in case he died before Betty.

The pastor began to read....

"My dear wife....God gave me the most incredible help-mate ever when He gave me you. Please, I know that you will miss me (but not my snoring). Rest assured I have a seat for you right at the table that has been prepared. We will be together again soon my love, very soon.

Now, Linda, you have always been the 'apple of my eye', well until the grandkids came, but you know what I mean."

Everyone laughed out loud.

"You are such an incredible mother and wife...I can tell you have learned well from your mother. Please don't cry for me, for I am in such a wonderful place. I know that it will be hard...but you are strong in the Lord and you can make it.

Take care of those precious grandchildren and remind them how much their Granddad loved them."

Linda and Paul grabbed each others' hand along with their children's hands.

I glanced over at Mark and saw his face. He knew he was next, and he was not sure what to expect. Mark's eyes were swollen from all the crying and I could see his worry.

Suddenly my hand was on top of his. He looked as shocked as I was. I did not even think about the gesture until after I had done it.

The pastor continued.....

"My son, Mark. Oh... how I love you. You are a hard worker and you take after me in so many ways, especially in the 'strong-willed' department.

Your children were my first grandchildren and I watched you become the most wonderful dad to them. I would like to think that was another way you took after me as well.

And son, always remember that the Father is not done with you yet."

I thought I should remove my hand at that point, but Mark just held it tighter.

The pastor continued with the letter and it held sweet words for me and Paul, Linda's husband. When he started reading to the grandchildren I almost could not contain myself. He always knew them so well and knew just what to say to each of them.

The service ended with a glorious old gospel song WHEN WE ALL GET TO HEAVEN. I could not help but smile. I knew that John was in heaven and seeing his Jesus. "A day of rejoicing" indeed.

The kids said their goodbyes and took me to the front of the room. One of the roses in the arrangement the kids had ordered for their grandfather had literally wilted since yesterday.

"Mom," said Matthew, "don't let that be our dad."

I could not believe that one of them had wilted, but that was exactly how Mark was feeling right now. Why was it my responsibility to help him feel any other way? *Because of my unconditional love daughter.*

CHAPTER 35
1981

The funeral ended and the church provided a lovely dinner. There was enough food to feed the entire town and then some. Mary Beth had seen Sam at the funeral with his "bosses" and invited them to eat as well.

Sam was thrilled to be eating "Mr. John's food." He was a joy and the kids loved talking to him. His smile and attitude were indeed contagious.

We all sat and visited with old friends and relatives. Soon it was time to leave, and Mark and I would go to our separate homes and things would go back to our "new normal".

"But this feels normal," I thought to myself. Although I knew it was never to be again....or was it? "What am I thinking?" I thought to myself. "My emotions are all caught up in this, I have to get a hold of myself."

"Mattie, please don't leave yet," Mark said as I started towards the exit. I had said my goodbyes to Linda, Peter and the kids. I had already given Betty a hug with a promise to have coffee very soon.

"Mattie, thank you so much for all you have done. I simply could not have made it through all of this without you and the kids by my side." He grabbed my hands and held them tight.

"Well, of course, the kids would be here for you," I said with a bit of a tremor in my voice.

"I know they would be...but nothing said you had to be here," Mark replied.

I started to say something, but instead, I said goodbye and made my exit. I got in the car and began to weep. I must be exhausted and emotionally drained, I thought to myself as I drove out of the parking lot.

The kids had decided that they would stay with their dad at Betty's. He had stayed at his mother's the last couple of days so he could help with the visitors that were coming in and out.

The kids were ready for their first night at their grand-mother's without Granddad. I could not say no to them. It was still summer and they needed their dad as much as he needed them.

I walked in the door and stepped on kibbles of food. As was typical, when poor Buster felt abandoned he left kib-bles of his food everywhere. Granted the last few days had been crazy, but ever since Mark had left he had done it so much more.

It seemed he missed him as much as I did. "What did I just say?" I spoke out loud. "Buster misses Mark as much as me?? I am exhausted." I headed back to the bathroom to get ready for bed.

I went through my normal bedtime routine. I read part of my novel, which normally helped me feel at least a little sleepy. Tonight was not going to be one of those nights that sleep came easily. I could not turn off my brain.

Why was I thinking about Mark? Oh, I had thought about Mark for many nights since the divorce, but not with the tenderness I felt tonight.

"It is sympathy," I mumbled out loud to Buster, who had been my visitor in bed every night for months now.

He just looked at me as if to say "No, I don't think so." I suggested he get off the bed immediately after that com-ment! He did not comply. He began licking my face.

After several hours of tossing back and forth, counting a baker's dozen of everything I served, I must have dozed off. But the next morning I remembered my dreams.

Everything I could remember had contained Mark. Mark when we first met, Mark on our first date, Mark when he asked me to marry him, Mark when the kids were born. I remembered Mark and I celebrating our anniversary and a birth of a grandchild. What??

"Oh boy, it will be so hard when the kids get married and have children," I said to myself. After all the crazy dreams from last night, I had an idea.

It had been months since I had taken the time to write in my journal. I had started writing when I was just a little girl, and more after my dad died. I was so young, but it felt good to write down my feelings.

My journals were my treasures. They were a place where I could write down my innermost feelings, my ideas for the bakery, my problems, and my prayers.

It had been a long time since I had done any of that. Without my journal, I would have made a psychologist a very rich individual.

I rummaged through my dresser drawer and found my longtime friend. I even found a new pen. A new pen was essential when writing new thoughts in my journal after a long time. Truly, I was like a kid in a candy shop. I loved a new pen with new pages and always had felt that way. The coffee was brewing and I was ready to sit for a while. I might even write down a prayer or two.

I was sitting on the back porch writing and drinking my second cup of coffee when I heard a car pull in the driveway. Buster's tail began to wag as he ran to the window. The kids came running in the door.

"Hey Mom!" they all chimed in at once. The two older children had plans for the day, as summer was winding down.

"Mom, I am going to the bakery with you today, right?" Michelle asked as she dropped her bag in the hallway where she always seemed to put it.

"Bag?" That seemed to be the reminder she needed each and every time to put it in her room! Oh how I love teens.

She was so interested in learning all she could about the bakery and the recipes. She reminded me so much of myself on those days that I could not wait to get to Aunt Esther's kitchen. Who knew, maybe Michelle would be running the bakery one day?

"Grandma Betty might come in for coffee today," said Michelle. Mark walked in behind the kids but still offered a polite knock at the door before entering.

That seemed so strange that he should knock before entering a home he had lived in for so many years, yet the gesture touched me somehow.

"Mattie, I am sorry...if you are busy," Mark offered.

"No, come in and have some coffee. I have been sitting on the back porch. I have a little bit of time before we need to get to the bakery."

"Man I miss that porch," he said with his head hanging down. "Mom said she was going to run by and see you sometime today. She was so appreciative of your support over the last several days," Mark whispered.

"Of course, your Mom is always welcomed at the bakery. Do you have another day off?"

"Yes, I told the guys that I needed to go over some papers with Mom and take her to town. But don't worry, I will just drop her off at the bakery." I looked at him with an expression that I did not recognize either.

164

"Well, thanks for the coffee and back porch offer, but I better get going if I am going to help Mom," Mark said as he headed for the door.

The kids gave him a hug and he began to walk out the door.

"Mark," I said. "Feel free to come in with your Mother today, I really don't mind." Mark smiled and headed down the steps.

"What on earth did I just do?" I sighed at my comment.

"Yes!" Michelle yelled as she hopped up the stairs two at a time. "Hey guys, I get to see Dad again at the bakery today." She sounded happier than I had heard her sound in ages. She was even whistling! I had not heard happiness like that from her in a very long time.

"Okay young lady, time to get ready if you are going to work with me." She left to get dressed.

"Put on something halfway decent dear one," I said with a smile on my face. "Hmmm, what should I put on? I might get to see Mark again."

WHERE ON EARTH were these thoughts coming from?

165

CHAPTER 36
1981

Michelle and I walked into the bakery. The morning crew had been there since 4 am and their jovial mood was noticeable. I liked to think that people liked working for me, although I know that the last few months I had not been the most pleasant person to be around.

Most of the crew understood why because of all that had gone on. I did not talk about it, after all, I was their boss, but people somehow found out what had happened, and why.

"Michelle is here!" shouted Norah to everyone in the kitchen.

"Hey girl, so glad you are here!" Tim yelled over the mixers.

Everyone loved Michelle and her caring personality and smile. People were always teaching her about the bakery routine and what they did there. And she loved it.

It was like my aunt's kitchen on a much grander scale. Mattie was so happy that Michelle enjoyed baking as much as she did. Oh, how she wished she could have met her great aunt.

Michelle was actually becoming a talent in the kitchen. And most importantly, she enjoyed it. I really felt like she would someday run the business.

It will be great to travel the world when we retire," Mattie thought to herself. "What on earth am I saying 'we' for? This is getting ridiculous. *I have a plan, sweet daughter.*

Mark and his mother came into the bakery around 9:30.

"Mom? Dad and Grandmother are here...can I give them one of the new pastries I just invented?" Michelle practically begged..

"I guess, but not sure we can put it on the board just yet kiddo," said Mattie.

"Mom......I know that! Daddy and Grandmother can be my guinea pigs," she winked as she brought out the blueberry pastry. One bite is all either of them needed to tell Michelle just how wonderful it was.

"We have a winner!" Mark announced as he raised Michelle's arm in victory.

Mattie sat down at the table with her ex-husband and her ex-mother-in-law. It felt so right. She had to get a hold of herself. This was not part of her "new normal."

"Betty, you look well rested today," Mattie said.

"Oh honey, I don't know what I would do without Mark....he has been such a Godsend. I am so grateful for such a wonderful, caring son."

That stung. Was he so wonderful and caring months ago when he was having an affair with the other woman? Suddenly I felt flushed and excused myself to the kitchen.

I honestly had not gotten mad like that since before the visit about Mark's dad. Of course, I hadn't. The circumstances forced me to forget about the truth. And I needed to remember it.

"Mom, honestly...why did you walk away from Dad and Grandmother so mad? What did they do?" Michelle asked as she walked back into the kitchen.

It seemed so unfair when the kids asked me why I did something. I did not want them to know what had happened and dishonor their father, but honestly....he was dishonorable! *Don't do it daughter. Control your tongue.*

"I just started to feel ill, so I thought I should get away from Grandmother. She doesn't need to take a chance and get anything." I told Michelle.

"Please tell them that I cannot come back out, but I will see them later. Tell your Grandmother that I love her."

Michelle replied..."but don't tell Dad that right?" and she stomped off into the dining area.

"What am I doing to my daughter? To our kids?" I thought. I walked back out to the dining area right before Mark and Betty were walking out the door.

"Mark, stop...I am sorry. I had no right to lash out at you. What's done is done. I know we have to move forward from here."

Mattie extended her hand. Mark shook it as strangers would shake upon meeting for the first time. Betty then gave Mattie a hug.

"Mom, Dad is going to take lunch to Sam like he promised. Can I go with him to the factory?"

"Sure," said Mattie. "A promise is a promise."

Mark and Michelle walked in the front door of the factory. There were a number of special needs adults that worked and trained from their group home.

"Mr. Mark, you made it again. I knew you would not forget. You are just like Mr. John, and I love you too." Sam gave Mark and Michelle a big hug.

"I won't forget you, Sam, I won't forget." They hugged Sam back and were on their way.

"Dad, there is something really special about Sam, isn't there?" Michelle said.

"Yes, sweetie, I think we could actually learn a lot from him," said Mark.

"Neat," she said as she slipped her thirteen-year-old hand into his like she did when she was four.

"We could learn a lot," he repeated.

CHAPTER 37
1981

Mark and Michelle picked up Mary Beth and Matthew for dinner. They laughed at their dad while they ate pizza, he was always making stupid jokes.

"Dad," Matthew said, becoming quite serious, "Do you think that you and mom will ever get back together? This is just wrong..us not being a family and all."

"Yeah, Dad, what is wrong with Mom? Why did she make you leave like that? What is wrong with her?" Mary Beth added.

"Kids, trust me, your Mom had a good reason to ask me to leave. I was wrong with so many things I did. I have an idea, let's just pray about it and see what happens."

"That is all I have been doing Dad. We talked about it at camp, we have talked about it between ourselves, and it seems like God isn't even listening." Matthew was frustrated. He paused as he was working on his third slice of pizza.

"Son, God hears everything you say to Him, but sometimes people make choices that are just wrong. But He can take bad things and make them good if we just trust Him."

"Wow…that just came from you Lord!" Mark was so grateful He was reading his Bible and trying to listen to the Lord now.

The kids went back to Mark's apartment to spend the night. They played a couple of board games and laughed some more. It wasn't long after they started a movie that they all were dozing off.

"Dad, I am going to bed," said Michelle. Soon they all were in their beds, their small, uncomfortable beds.

"They should be in their own bedrooms," Mark murmured as he kissed them all good night.

The morning seemed to come fast as Mark fixed breakfast. He would never get used to living in this apartment. Even when the kids were there, something...no someone was missing. And he wasn't just talking about Buster. He missed Mattie horribly.

"Dad, I don't feel so good," said Michelle as she walked into the kitchen.

"Let me feel your head kiddo. My gosh, you are burning up!" "Go get back in bed and I will bring you some aspirin for that fever."

"Dad, please call Mom, I feel awful."

"All right honey, I will call her as soon as I get your medicine."

"What's wrong with sis?" said Matthew.

"She hasn't been feeling good for a while," said Mary Beth.

"She hasn't said anything to me about feeling bad," Mark said to the kids.

"She did not want to tell you guys because so much has been going on. You know Michelle."

Mark dialed Mattie's number. "Mattie, hey it is me. I am ok. But there is something wrong with Michelle. She is burning up with fever and the kids said she has been feeling bad for several days. I know, she has not said a thing to me either. Sure, come on over." Mark hung up the phone. "Your mom is on her way."

Mattie knocked on the door. "Why is Mom knocking?" said Matthew.

"Dufus, she doesn't live here," replied Mary Beth. Matthew threw a pillow off the couch at his sister. He barely missed his mom as she walked in the door.

170

"Well, I see some things are just the same here as they are at home. Where's Michelle?"

It had only been about 40 minutes, so the aspirin probably should have had time to work.

"Sweetie, how long have you been feeling bad?' Mattie leaned down to feel Michelle's forehead.

"For a while, my stomach hurts right here." Michelle pointed to the lower right side of her abdomen.

"She did not eat a lot of pizza last night," said Mark.

"Oh man, I feel sick," and Michelle got out of bed and took off for the bathroom.

"What should we do Mattie?" Mark asked.

"Well, I don't want to think the worse, but with her fever, the pain and now her being sick…it could be a stomach virus or her appendix. Let's not take any chances. Let's take her on to the ER."

By the time they got to the ER Michelle was in excruciating pain. After the doctors examined her and did some tests they told Mark and Mattie that they would have to operate.

"You got her here just in time, her appendix is about to burst," said the doctor. After telling Michelle she would feel better soon they wheeled her back to surgery. This was too much and Mattie simply broke down.

"Oh my gosh, we have been so wrapped up in our lives that we missed our child being so sick. She had not been feeling good and I did not even notice it. What kind of mom am I?" Mattie held on to Mark's arm.

"Mattie, I am the one who has been selfish…..she is going to be all right. The doctor said we got here just in time," Mark said with all the comfort he had left in him.

"Mattie, I am so sorry for everything I put you and the kids through. You have no idea" Mark whispered.

As they sat near each other in the waiting room the kids came in with Betty, Aunt Linda…and Sam!

"She is going to be all right, she should be out of surgery soon," said Mattie as she hugged all of them.

"Sam, what are you doing here?" said Mark.

"My friends Mary Beth and Matthew came with Miss Betty and Miss Linda to bring my lunch. I did not have to work very long today, so I asked where Mr. Mark was and they said my friend Michelle was sick, so I asked if I could come to visit with them. Everyone said yes, so here I am!" his smile was as big as his bear hug.

"This is just what Mr. John always wanted. Everyone loving and hugging each other like Jesus told us to do. He said that Miss Mattie and Mr. Mark would be kissing again one day. He just knew it!"

Everyone in the room looked at each other, then at Sam and soon burst out laughing.

"That would be my John," Betty said with a big smile.

"Let's pray for Michelle," said Sam "We have to pray for Michelle until she gets better!"

Everyone in the waiting room held hands in a huge circle while Sam prayed.

"Jesus, you are my best friend. Now my other friend is sick. Her name is Michelle and I want you to make her better. The doctors are smart, so I know she will be as good as new soon. And please tell my friend, Mr. John hello up there. I know you seen him already. Thank you, Jesus. Amen."

There was not a dry eye as Sam finished up his prayer. Even the other people in the waiting room had bowed their heads as sweet Sam spoke to Jesus from the bottom of his heart.

The doctor came out to report all went well with Michelle and she would be in recovery soon. They really had gotten her there just in time. She would indeed be as good as new in a couple of weeks.

"Thank the Lord," Sam's grin could not have been any wider!

CHAPTER 38
1981

Michelle came home from the hospital and was able to start school on time. She was feeling so much better.

Even though she had not been able to spend as much time in the bakery as she wanted, she had added to her recipe notebook and had plenty of new things she wanted to try. Mattie did not realize how bad she had looked until she looked better.

Mark had been by a lot to check in on Michelle and a couple of times he had stayed for dinner. It was just like old times. Well, kind of. Mark was different. He led them in the dinner prayer and a few times talked to them about some Bible passage he had been studying.

"Could he truly be a changed man?" thought Mattie one evening when he left. *People can change when they surrender to me.*

The days seem to fly by as summer turned to fall. Football season was in full gear, homecoming around the corner.

"I have to clean up this office," Mattie said out loud to Buster after the kids headed to school. "I have let that pile of mail get high again." Buster just wagged his tail.

At least my journal was in use again. It had helped me so much to put my thoughts in written forms and I had started writing scripture as well. Truth be known, my journal had become a "prayer journal" of sorts.

I had actually prayed for "our" lives, mine and Mark's... together. I never thought I would even consider praying for that.....and I did not actually think it would come to pass. I had too much to get through before I could even consider forgiveness. *Seventy times seventy.*

I stared at the two piles on my desk as if they would straighten themselves up on their own. One of the piles looked like it was a transplant from the kitchen table. That stack had been accumulating for months, and with Michelle's recent health scare and the onset of school, it was worse than the usual accumulating piles.

"I hope there are not any bills in this stack!" I brought the trash can to the edge of the desk.

Soon my trash can was full and I was at the end of the second stack.

"Strange, I remember this envelope." The large envelope with the shaky handwriting looked so important months ago. But somehow it had gotten pushed to the bottom of the pile and was never opened.

"It is time to open this mystery envelope," I said to Buster as the phone rang. "Buster, watch that envelope and don't let it leave your sight."

One phone call about a wedding order soon turned into another call from a lady planning her parents' 50th Wedding Anniversary.

Each call was from family or friends and they liked to talk to me in person rather than calling the bakery and giving their orders. That was always fine with me because I knew that without their business I would not be as successful as I had been.

As I was about to walk into the office the phone rang again…this time about providing cookies for the football team for their "pre-game" dinner on Thursday night.

"Sure, no problem," I replied to the head of the football dinner committee.

"Are you kidding me? I said as I sat down the phone and it rang yet again. "I am going to have to get a line in this office if the phone is going to ring all the time."

"Mattie, hey it is Mark...I was wondering if the parent called you about the cookies?"

"Yes, and thanks for letting me answer the question on that. I truly appreciate it," said Mattie with sincerity.

Before the conversation was over she had actually agreed to have dinner with Mark...alone.

"What am I doing?" Mattie finally got off the phone.

"Now where was I?" Mattie said to Buster as she walked back into the office. "Oh yeah, the letter. The mysterious letter that keeps getting away from me."

Buster begged to be picked up. "Not yet boy, not yet." I finally tore open the envelope and began to read the shaky handwritten letter.....

Little did I know...

CHAPTER 39
1981

"Little did I know" …..that seemed an understatement now. My hand trembled as I reread the letter.

"Dearest Mattie,

I am sure you don't remember me, but I was friends with your sweet mother for years. We attended the Baptist church together. I sat with my husband and mother toward the front of the church for years.

You were always the sweetest little girl and you were so polite. We did not talk a lot, but I thought so much of your mother and father.

We had a quilting circle for years. One afternoon it was just your mother and I and we began to talk and compare stories about our children and our lives.

As your mother talked, I began to understand the details of your birth."

The details of my birth? What hadn't my mother told me?? I continued to read.

"Your adoption was similar to my own adoption. For some reason, your mother did not want to share the truth with you. I disagreed with her and it was not my place to tell her what to do.

But my adoption had been a huge secret for years and it hurt me so much when I found out from someone who was sharing it with me just to be vengeful. It cost my family a lot of love loss and valuable time together.

I decided that if something ever happened to your mother that I would share with you what I knew to be true. I have prayed about it for years, and out of sheer respect for your mother, I did not share it while she was still alive.

Your mother was a wonderful person and just did not want to see you hurt in any way. She simply wanted to protect you. She felt like so many years had passed without the truth. She thought she would lose you."

My hands continued to shake as I finished the letter. I read it over and over at least three more times.

I was raised by Anne and Oscar for the first ten years of my life. They were the most wonderful parents that a child could ever have. They loved me and taught me about God and His love.

Mother, Daddy, and Aunt Esther always lived a surrendered life in front of me and loved on everyone around them. My father died when I was just ten years old and my mother raised me all alone after that.

I often felt alone, but now I see that wasn't really the case. I had Joseph, Ruby Kay, and Little Annie to play with and watch over me.

Mother was never alone either and did have some help from her best friend, Aunt Esther. She was always very special to me. She taught me so much.

Aunt Esther always shared many stories of love and kindness with me as we worked in her kitchen. She treated me as though I was one of her own. And I guess I truly was.

I was the unexpected gift.

Now I had to wonder...were there more of those to come?

Note from the Author

My prayer is that this novel will encourage you in your life today. You may not be experiencing the same problems as Mattie and Mark, Esther and Thomas or Oscar and Anne, but most certainly there are some type of issues that have occurred in your life in the past, the present or will in the future.

Always remember what Jesus said:

"I have told you these things, so that you may have peace. In this world, you <u>will</u> have trouble. But take heart! I have overcome the world." **John 16:33 NIV**

Friends, He has overcome the world! That is good news!

Be sure and watch for~
Book 2-*Take Heart*
Book 3-*Overcome*
Coming soon from the *Unexpected Gift* Series.

About the Cover

My husband is a gifted artist. I have a tendency to ask him to draw or paint something on the spur of the moment. Our eldest son actually took the picture. My husband painted it.

The painting is called "The Smokies through the Pines." I thought it would make a fabulous cover based on one of the settings in the book.

He paints and sketches and loves to do commissioned work for people. His talent is indeed a gift from God and I am so glad in his retirement he has been able to pursue this lifelong love.

He claims 1 Corinthians 10:31 and puts it on every piece that leaves the studio. His work can be found at a local mercantile or online at:

www.southernillinoismercantileco.com

https://www.facebook.com/aaallgaierartwork/

https://www.instagram.com/aaallgaierartwork/

About the Author

T. W. Allgaier writes from her heart. She truly believes that encouraging others in their daily lives is a calling on her life.

She has written several short magazine articles, devotions for a Ukrainian magazine and maintained a blog for several years.

She taught special needs students for fifteen years, and homeschooled her two sons for ten years. She has been an Assistant Director for a crisis pregnancy center, taught Bible studies, and has been a speaker at several Woman's Conferences. She also has worked as a radio announcer at a local contemporary radio station for several years.

She has been married almost 39 years to her high school sweetheart and has two adult sons and daughters-in-law. She has just recently become a grandmother for the first time. It is indeed a love like no other.

You can find her blog, "Encouragement for Today" or follow her on Facebook at:

www.yelobrd777.com

www.theyellowbirdlife.com

https://www.facebook.com/yelobrd777/

You are welcome to leave a book review on Amazon.

If you would like to be added to our mailing list for updates on upcoming books and other neat things, please click this link or send an email to
theyellowbirdlife@gmail.com

Thank you for taking time out of your busy schedule to read this book. I know it is not perfect, but my prayer is that you hear The Father's heart. Always rest in the arms of His peace, grace and love.

Made in the USA
Las Vegas, NV
15 January 2022